TALL
TALES
FROM THE
TALL
PINES

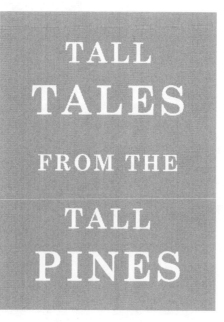

Christian P. Potholm

Down East Books

Camden, Maine

This is a work of fiction. Names, characters, places, and incidents either are the product of the author's imagination or are used fictitiously. Any resemblance to actual persons, living or dead is entirely coincidental.

Published by Down East Books
An imprint of The Rowman & Littlefield Publishing Group, Inc.
4501 Forbes Boulevard, Suite 200, Lanham, Maryland 20706
www.rowman.com

Unit A, Whitacre Mews, 26-34 Stannary Street, London SE11 4AB,
United Kingdom

Distributed by NATIONAL BOOK NETWORK

British Library Cataloguing in Publication Information Available

Library of Congress Cataloging-in-Publication Data

Potholm, Christian P., 1940– author.
  Tall tales from the tall pines / Christian P. Potholm.
     pages cm
  ISBN 978-1-60893-471-3 (pbk. : alk. paper) — ISBN 978-1-60893-472-0 (electronic)
    1. Hunting—Maine—Anecdotes. 2. Fishing—Maine—Anecdotes. 3. Outdoor life—Maine—Anecdotes. 4. Maine—Anecdotes. I. Title.
  SK85.P67 2015
  799.09741—dc23   2015021379

∞™ The paper used in this publication meets the minimum requirements of American National Standard for Information Sciences—Permanence of Paper for Printed Library Materials, ANSI/NISO Z39.48-1992.

Printed in the United States of America

Contents

Dedication

To Ezra Smith, Livey Huntley, and Old Rope,
Grand Men of the Great North Woods

And

To Papa John Quinlan, whose final dying gift
was to unleash the telling of these tales.

"Fiction reveals truth that reality obscures."

RALPH WALDO EMERSON

"I have scarcely exaggerated a detail of this curious and absurd adventure. It occurred almost exactly as I have stated it."

MARK TWAIN, *Roughing It*

"Truth is so hard to tell, it sometimes needs fiction to make it plausible."

FRANCIS BACON, *Apologies*

"Such events happened on the borderline of fable, the unmarked frontier between Washoe and fantasy."

BERNARD DEVOTO, *Across the Wide Missouri*

Introduction

"Hilarious Hunting Tales"

AS A MAINE GUIDE for twenty years and a hunter and fisherman since childhood, Chris Potholm knows the woods and waters of Maine from the coast to the North Woods. He brings it all to life with humorous tales, astonishing and intriguing characters, and real-life dialogue in *Tall Tales from the Tall Pines*. Yes, these are authentic, how-they-talk, what-they-do, Maine hunting and fishing stories with Maine Guides, wardens, sports and gun shop owners all presented in full blossom. These tales are also hilarious. My wife Lin would often ask me why I was laughing out loud by the fire when I read them.

Boy, can Chris tell a good story!

Truth be told, some of these deceptively "plain tales" are based on the hunting and angling experiences that Chris and I have enjoyed together or watched unfold before our very eyes. He's embellished them a bit here and there (and changed the names to protect the guilty as well as the innocent no doubt!) and added a lot of humor while bringing together the best episodes with some new characters. But they are right on target in giving the reader a true sense of what happens when the likes of Snappy Jack and Big Gus go "afield" into the real Maine outdoor, the one we all know and love—with all its rough edges and surprising dimensions.

Originally I had hoped to contribute some stories of my own to this book, but I just could not keep up with Chris's prolific pace of writing, nor could I come close to the wonderful style and characters he's given us. So I opted to write this introduction and contribute a few ideas (some damn fine ones if I do say so myself!) to get him started on stories and then to tell him which of his characters I wanted to hear more about. He would email me one or two stories at a time and I'd stop whatever I was doing and read them immediately, laughing and admiring the way he was able to present outdoor experiences in such an elaborate, entertaining, and authentic way.

You will surely select your favorite characters in this collection—mine is Willimina, for whom the NRA is way, way too liberal. In "William Kicks Serious Butt" she really comes to life, probably because the story is loosely based on some real life experiences of some of my own relatives. You may choose Big Gus, a Maine Guide who Chris describes as "refined." There are not many guides who drive Land Rovers but the ones that do, well, they take their special, rare shotguns to heart just the way old Gus does! The accounts of Gus shooting with the Queen and saving a young girl in Merrymeeting Bay will have you smiling for days. Incidentally, Gus also has a morbid fear of eels and getting his feet wet!

Or you may root for Zapper Johnson, the Swedish lobsterman and hunter, who is in and out of the law, but a hell of an outdoorsman and somebody you'd like with you on an extended hunting trip. Or you might not. That probably will depend on whether or not you've ever been on the wrong side of the law, however briefly. But if you're ever "Jumping Through the Junipers" after snowshoe hares in the remote Maine townships north and east of Bangor, you'll want someone like Zapper beside you, of that I'm more than sure. Zapper's brother Pepper is an out-and-out outlaw. I sure hope you don't identify with him, except perhaps for his love of Whoopee pies!

But the real Maine has all these characters in it and lots more. They don't often make the sporting journals, but everybody who has spent a lot of time hunting or fishing knows exactly where they can find a couple of Chris's characters—within only a few moments' notice out in the field—or in town bragging about their latest exploits, some of which may actually turn out to be true.

Hell, just go to a Moxie parade, or any hunter's breakfast in Waldo or Aroostook counties—or any other counties for that matter—and you'll recognize half the characters in the book, just by the way they talk and the tales they tell. Their dialogue rings true from start to finish.

You may learn a few things from these stories too. About the fish and the animals we seek when we all go afield. About the real Wild Wild East that is Maine. There is a lot of accumulated hunting and fishing wisdom here, sometimes hidden in the free flowing dialogue and dry humor. You know the author has gotten his deer and his moose and his bear and his "pork-e-pine." Just wait until you read the story about the moose uterus. True. All true.

"Duck Feathers Destroy a Friendship" is certain to be a classic for it captures not only the nature of real duck hunting and the Maine Guide's love of the creatures he or she hunts, but also the competition among guides for sports and the powerful story of how self-promotion can lead to revenge and disaster.

And "Blizzard Buck" illuminates that all important component of the out of doors, "Lady Luck." We all like to think we're successful out in the woods and on the lakes and streams due to our mastery of outdoor lore. But in deer hunting, as in love, it is clearly much better to be lucky than good (are you listening, Lin? I was damn lucky!). Chris knows this and captures its true essence. Then "The Curse of the Beaver Lady" will have you chuckling from beginning to end, whether you like beavers or not. Or even if you've not had "beaver flu" or met a librarian like Phoebe Prendergast (although just about every small town has one!).

I'll bet you a moose burger on that.

These are not your ordinary hunting stories either. I guarantee you have never, ever read an account of a deer hunting camp like "Snow Dance," not in *Sports Afield*, not in *Grey's Sporting Journal*, not even in the *Maine Sportsman*. I can still smell that camp and taste its food and feel the roiling emotions of the hunters and guides as the rain pours down. This is what Hemingway called "the true gen."

These are stories to be savored, read to your children and grandchildren, even picked up on many a cold winter evening to be read again by the fire.

And don't be embarrassed if you laugh out loud.

I did.

Start savoring.

GEORGE SMITH
Mount Vernon, Maine

Eighteen-Year Executive Director, Sportsman's Alliance of Maine, author of the highly acclaimed *A Life Lived Outdoors*, columnist for the *Kennebec Journal*, *Waterville Sentinel*, and *Maine Sportsman*, and host of TV talk show *Wildfire*

chapter
one

One Happy Sport

"**S**NAP, what was the name of that guy from Tennessee, one of the first sports we ever guided?" asked Big Gus. We were sitting by his fire, enjoying the sense of well-being that comes from being warm on a cold December day and sharing stories of the out of doors on a day when you're glad you don't have to be out of doors. Of course, drinking Gus's fifteen-year-old Macallan didn't hurt either. Big Gus and I had been guiding sports in Maine for twenty years or more and we had a few stories to tell, even to each other, though I'd forgotten more than a few of them. But this one tickled me for some reason.

"Damn, I don't know, wasn't it Billy Bob or one of those funny Southern names?" I said, "Damned if I know." Gus stared into the fire for a while, then chuckled. "Jimbo, that's what it was, Jimbo Clayton. He was a pip."

"Was he ever," I answered. "We worked hard for that money. Learned to give the client what he wanted no matter how weird too."

1

And weird it was. Jimbo had written us saying he wanted to go sea ducking "and shoot some other critters" although he didn't say which ones. We figured he'd love the wild action of sea ducking and the big bag limits. A real Maine adventure in the Wild, Wild East. We set up a date and when he arrived, we put him up in a nice local motel and told him to be ready at 5 a.m. the next morning. And he was. Many sports need to be waked up and pushed out the door on their merry way, but not Jimbo. When we arrived, he was dressed and ready to go, if anything straining at the bit. Of course we had to add to his wardrobe a couple of sweaters and waterproof outer pants. Those ledges were often coated with rime ice and cold as hell with a northwest wind.

In fact, what with the long boat ride out to sea, Jimbo *was* freezing by the time we got to the outer ledges and set him up behind some rocks. Gus and I had not yet gotten over being surprised at how the sports would just sit there and let you do all the work, setting the decoys and piling up the drift wood and dry kai. We were always glad to be working ourselves and getting the blood moving rather than sitting there getting colder and colder waiting for the action to begin. Gus was, as always, a little bummed by the fact that only the head decoy in each of our strings was a fine George Soule creation, the rest being just Clorox jugs with a slash of black paint. "Embarrassing" he called it, more than once although the eiders never did complain.

But then, eiders and scoters don't seem to have the intelligence of black ducks or mallards when it comes to decoys, or maybe it's just the perspective since they don't usually fly as high as black ducks and mallards and swimming so low a flash of white among the waves is enough to attract them.

Anyway, it was a gorgeous day with rafts of eider and scoter all around the ledges, gorging on the mussel beds in the bay as the tide continued to drop. Once they started flying with the lobster boats arriving and other hunters shooting, it was like the battle of Waterloo, guns going off all over the place and the ducks flying in long rows only a few feet off the wave tops.

Jimbo quickly became agitated. "Look at all those ducks, look at all those ducks," he exclaimed, "how do I know which one to shoot?"

"Not sure it makes a lot of difference," remarked Gus, looking at me with a funny look that said "Whose the hell's idea was this anyway?"

"But I want a special one," Jimbo said.

"A special one?" Gus replied, more than a little perplexed. "A special sea duck?"

"Yeh, I'm only going to shoot one. I want it to be special."

Well that was a first, here we were in the middle of great rafts of sea ducks, hundreds of them flying wildly around, long rows skimming over the wave tops, a lot within shotgun range already as the other gunners put them up flight after flight.

"One eider?" Gus repeated as if he'd missed something important.

"I've got a nice collection of critters at home," Jimbo said. "One of each. A man don't need more than one of each, know what I mean?"

Well, I didn't know what he meant and Gus didn't either but Gus was always quick on the uptake so he drew himself up and scanned an incoming flight. "That one. That one right in the middle of the line. That's as good an eider as I've seen in years."

Jimbo jumped up and fired his 12-gauge twice right into the middle of the line. Luckily a big white plumed male dropped into the sea and I paddled out to retrieve it. "Sure is a nice one," I said, getting into the spirit of things. "It's some handsome a duck I can tell you that. Don't know when I've ever seen one as big and pretty as this one. Sure is cunnin'."

Well Jimbo was pleased as punch. Lord wasn't he happy, jumping up on first one leg and then the other. "Got him.

Got him." Even when he slipped on the icy seaweed and fell down, he kept his grin and got up. "Gollee Gollee Hot damn, hot damn, the Mrs. is sure going to like to see this one stuffed. It's a beauty. It's a real beauty."

Gus and I ooh'd and ah'd some over the dead eider and then Gus declared, "Well it's time to get some breakfast and hot coffee." As we were picking up the long string of decoys, a number of which were now all tangled together and coated with ice, Gus whispered, "That's a first."

"Well," I allowed, "it'll be nice and warm at Becky's."

So there we were a half hour later, sitting in a nice warm booth, ordering stacks of blueberry pancakes with all the fixings of a full hunter's breakfast with many cups of boiling hot coffee, not sure what we were going to do next and fending off questions from Becky and her staff, questions like, "You boys are off to a late start, aren't you?" Gus, who always cared for appearances, raised an eyebrow and allowed as how we were actually some early. "Got our limit very quickly; Jimbo here is a real good shot."

About halfway through the meal, once Jimbo got over the disappointment of there being no grits to go with his blueberry pancakes, I finally got up nerve to ask him what critters he wanted to hunt next.

"Only one critter," he said, the butter and syrup glistening attractively in his beard. "I really want a pork e pine. One of them big northern pork e pines."

"A porcupine?" I repeated slowly. "A porcupine?"

"Well," said Gus, "they can be tricky. Hard to find this time of year. Why don't we see if we can get you a nice buck instead. The deer will be moving some good in this cold."

"Nope, I got a deer head on the wall at home. A nice little three pointer, one antler broken off. Real cute. No, I want a pork e pine. You guys are Maine Guides, I know you can find me a nice pork e pine. I hear tell they grow pretty damn big up here."

"Holy shit, Snap," said Gus when we were alone in the men's room. "Where the hell are we going to get a "pork-e-pine" in the middle of deer season?"

"Beats the hell out of me, Gus, but I think apple orchards are our only hope. Farmers don't like porcupines gnawing at their trees."

"Yeh, but most of them take care of that problem on their own."

"Well we haven't got any other bright ideas," he continued. "You take Jimbo out to some orchards and we'll get some grub at that sub place in Bowdoinham and compare notes. You might get lucky. In the meantime, I'll drive around and ask a few farmers if they've seen any."

The morning that followed was a bad dream. I dragged Jimbo from orchard to orchard. Traipsing through fields laced with cow manure and getting scolded by crows. The farmers were polite but "Sure, take a look but I ain't seen any sign of them varmints, not on my farm" was pretty much the standard refrain.

The bad news was we saw no porcupines that morning, and no signs of any either. The good news was Jimbo was extremely tired by noon and anxious to get grub. We met up with Gus and got a sub and a mess of corn chips and a beer and sat by the Cathance River to eat lunch. We told Gus we'd struck out but he said he had an idea. "Old Man Kerensky, he's got a lot of apple trees and he's always messing around with his milk cows, 'No time to hunt boys' he always says. We'll go ask him."

So we hit Kerensky's place early that afternoon. He had been a soldier in the Czarist army and escaped during the Russian Revolution, somehow bringing out his army rifle. But he never bothered to sight it in so he missed a lot of shots, except when he killed one of his sick milk cows and he gunned at that real close, as in three inches close.

When we arrived, there he was up on the roof of his barn, wailing away with a big hammer. Now, Kerensky is hard to understand even in the best of times. This day he was in rare form, gesturing wildly and gabbing away as he pointed to the orchard when Gus asked him if he had any problems with porcupines.

"Goddamn right, goddamn right, big porcupine, big fella, eat my apple trees. You fix him good. You fellahs fix him good, I fix you up with good prime beeve meat, you becha. You becha quick."

So off we trudged across his fields. There were miles of them and it seemed eons before we got to the orchard. Truth be told, it was an apple orchard in serious decline. Hadn't been pruned in years. Lots of wormy apples lying around. A ton of deer had been in and out, eating the apples and even throwing up some of the green ones.

It was a chore avoiding smashed apples and deer droppings and throw-up but we finally got Jimbo set in a tree and we went off to look for the porcupine. Kerensky was right, there was porcupine sign everywhere. There was chewed bark, tracks, the odd quill lying here and there and lots of that hard roundish scat they get in the winter when they are eating so much tough bark. And the smell, what a putrid odor.

Porcupines aren't subtle and neither is their scent, it's urine-like without the sweetish suggestion of skunk. Overall, Nature had made porcupines pretty stupid but pretty cocky what with all those quills and that really nasty smell. They also make a funny little shuffling sound as they move along and pretty soon we heard one. We looked and looked through the trees and finally saw a big old blackish porcupine ambling along without a care in the world about 50 yards away.

"Snap, you go back and get our sport, I'll keep the glasses on him," said Gus, and off I went, running like a shot. In fact I was so excited, I tripped over a root and fell down, causing Gus to laugh but he turned away so I wouldn't see the full extent of it. He's polite that way. Anyway, I finally got Jimbo's attention and he shimmied out of the tree and beat feet over to us.

"That's a king porcupine right over by that tree beyond Gus. A real beauty," I said. But before I could add, "I think you can get closer," Jimbo unleashed not just one barrel but two of the 12-gauge. "Boom. Boom." At the same time I was ducking a downpour of wizened apples, victims of Jimbo's shooting high. The sounds crashed across the valley. "I think you missed him," Gus said, unnecessarily I thought, because the porcupine was now ambling on down the trail picking up speed as he did.

"I'll get him," Jimbo called out as he ran after the porcupine, reloading as he went. This time he got within about twenty feet and then fired both barrels again. The porcupine expired on the spot and Jimbo began jumping up and down again, doing his little Southern victory dance. "Gollee Gollee I got him. I got him. What a shot. Did you see how fast he was moving? What a shot."

Both Gus and I allowed as how it was a terrific shot and we carried his gun and cartridge bag back to the truck while Jimbo carefully picked up the critter and carried him along, murmuring softly, "What a shot."

When we got to Old Man Kerensky's he was still up on the barn roof but when he saw we had the porcupine, he slid down the ladder and raced over. "Some good. Some fine damn good. I give you beeve to celebrate. Damn fine shot. Big beeve." Nothing would do but what we had to go into the dark, dank and really funky smelling barn with Old Man Kerensky and Jimbo doing a little jig in tandem along the way.

There, hanging from one of the rafters was one of his old milk cows. It wasn't clear from what it had expired, but Old Kerensky grabbed a big butcher knife and started hacking off one of the haunches. "You take. You take. Frigging good shot. Good beeve, I tell you, best beeve. You take. Sum bitch, good shot." He wrapped the meat in newspaper and gave it to Jimbo whose face lit up like a Christmas tree.

We thanked Old Kerensky and headed out.

That night Jimbo drove south with one eider, one porcupine, and quarter of a milk cow all packed nicely in ice.

One happy sport.

"Christ," said Gus after he departed, "he'll probably be back next year looking for a seal and a skunk."

So we were some relieved then when Jimbo Clayton later wrote us to thank us and said he was sorry, but the next fall he was heading south for his annual hunt. "I want to shoot a nice little alligator. Mama wants one for the sitting room."

Jumping through the Junipers with Sandy Andy

THE FIRST thing you have to know about Little Robert was that he had a younger brother named Big Robert as well as four other brothers, so his name never seemed quite right. You also should know that Big Robert wasn't his father's name either, for he was known simply as Robert. Now Robert himself was a legendary raiser of beagles and to have a Robert-raised running bitch was to be in an elite company in the Pine Tree State.

The problem was, of course, that Robert wouldn't sell one of his beagles to just anyone. I know because I once tried to buy one. He asked a million questions when I called him and he got all shirty when I said I was a Maine Guide and liked to hunt a lot of different things. "No way, Mr. Adams," he said righteously. "These dogs need to go to a good home. Someone who only hunts bunnies." So I never got one of his prize running bitches. But I did get to hunt with one of them, the legendary Sandy Andy.

Back to Little Robert. It wasn't that he was actually little. In fact he was about six feet tall. And it also wasn't that his Big Robert brother was older. He wasn't. Little Robert was the first born in the family, and taller than most of his brothers and had a son named Robby. ("Thank God," many said.) Robby hunted a lot as a small boy but later when he bought a Dairy Queen franchise he stopped having a lot of time to hunt. Still as Little Robert told us, while it was sad Robby could only go once in a while, since he took $100,000 a year out of that place and had a lot of cute high school girls working for him, he didn't feel too bad about things.

So it remained (and remains I must say) a mystery why Little Robert was called "little," although some wags among the guides often made jokes about the different reasons he was called Little Robert. Now not all of them were sexual in nature; but most probably were if you actually totaled them all up. It's fair to say that not all outdoorsmen are very subtle. But Little Robert did smoke a huge pipe (you could always tell where he was on stand by the smoke signals rising above the thick bunny brush like he was signaling somebody on a distant ridge or something), so maybe this time those jokes got it right.

Anyway, Little Robert had as fine a pack of rabbit hounds as anybody in the state and it was considered a real treat and honor to be invited along on one of his hunts. Watching the snowshoe or varying hares hopping along out ahead of the dogs was always exciting. Not that you shot a lot of hares you understand, when you were with Little Robert and his pack. In fact, Little Robert frowned on shooting a lot of bunnies at all. Truly any.

"The idea," he said, "the whole idea is the music, to stand in the woods and listen to the serenade. It's better than that symphony down in Portland." Since hares usually run in long ellipses (not circles) and when the hounds were on them and running well, there were natural crescendos and dimming of sounds as the hares ran into thick swamp or up over ridges. It really does have a magical sound in the crisp winter air, made even better if you chose a spot where you could actually watch the hare bounding out in front of the dogs, stopping and listening and then bounding off when they continued to close.

No, the main reason to hunt with Little Robert was to watch his best dog, Sandy Andy, run through the woods. Hop actually because Sandy Andy was an old dog with only three legs after she lost one to cancer. But boy, could she track hares. "Slow and steady and not afraid of junipers," said Little Robert. "And she makes great music." Hares, you see, like to eat juniper, and the thick, knarly knots of wild juniper make for great places to hide and some dogs don't hunt junipers well.

But Sandy Andy, slow and steady and always pausing to get her balance, would bounce right into the thickest junipers and never let go of that scent. She loved junipers. The younger dogs might burst ahead from time to time but often they'd get confused for a while and Sandy Andy would catch up. As Zapper Johnson rightly said, "Sandy Andy really ought to have been called 'Finished' because when she got on a scent, that hare was finished." Of course I pointed out the hare was only finished if Little Robert was allowing any shooting for the pot that day.

Now hares with their big feet leave a fair amount of scent all winter long but in March, when there is the equivalent of spring skiing—cold nights, warmer days—the hare scent holds best on the somewhat wet (but not too wet) snow. So there we were on that gorgeous March Saturday. Little Robert and Robbie, Zapper and myself plus Little Robert's four dogs and Zapper's ill trained but very musical dog, Patsy. Now Zapper was a big Swedish guy, massive back, massive hands, a slow way of speaking and a hell of a hunter. He could go all day tracking a deer or in this case cutting off hares like nobody's business. He'd run through the cedar swamps like they were tartan tracks.

Zapper is like a lot of guys in rural Maine. He's a part-time lobsterman and can dig clams when he has to or if the price is up. He's also a carpenter when there's work and he also sells wood out of his barn and in season, bait fish. There was talk that in his younger days he had been in the antique acquiring business, but that was never proven. He did travel a lot in the woods so he could have come upon a chair or painting or TV or other oddments along one of the various winding trails he frequented, especially on some of the larger islands in the bay.

Zapper was a hell of a shot too, but that wasn't how he got his name. When he was just out of trade school and convinced he could do anything he wanted, he decided to add "electrical contractor" to his title of carpenter but that career line never developed much after he nearly electrocuted his helper by not following—ignoring really—the electrical code. Still he always said hooking up wires was not "racket science." I always enjoyed hunting with Zapper. He was a man of few words but when he spoke it was usually with assurance like, "There ain't no damn bunnies in this swamp."

I guess I can also say that Zapper had a fondness for beer. Whenever we hunted the big Swede always had a six-pack strapped to his belt. While the rest of us drank coffee or hot chocolate on the breaks, Zapper would pop open a cold one and get refreshed no matter what the temperature. I once asked him if he didn't think he drank too much. "Nope," he said with a flat calm that defied qualification. "Nope, I never drink more than a case a day. Ever."

Zapper was also a legend in the community for his firmness when dealing with his wife, Zelda, a first generation Swedish lass herself. One story had Zapper coming home from two weeks in a deer camp and being served macaroni and cheese for dinner by Zelda. "What a christly insult that was," he said as he stalked out of the house after overturning the macaroni bowl in a big huff. "A man spends a couple of weeks eating venison tenderloin for every meal and then to be served this friggin' stuff when he comes home. What the hell is the matter with that woman. It's enough to drive a man to drink," he explained as he headed back to camp on principle.

Not surprising, Zelda eventually went back to Sweden on a vacation, met a nice man—a dentist in Malmo—and stayed on to eventually marry him. "He's a non-hunter! A non-drinker!!" she wrote on the wedding announcement. Her handwriting seemed light and joyful. "And is happy with macaroni" was the unwritten subtext.

Anyway, that gorgeous day passed quickly, the dogs chased a lot of bunnies and the music was superb and we had nobody along to shoot the spares, let alone the pursued hares. Sandy Andy was in amazing form. There was a huge old meadow, now overgrown with juniper bushes and the other faster dogs came through it in a flash, flushing a big buck hare out of the middle and chasing it hell bent for leather off to the north.

I looked at Little Robert and indicated we should head east to intercept the hare but he shook his head and cupped his ear. Sandy Andy was coming along slowly but making very strong noises. She came into the field and began jumping through the junipers, stopping here and there and doubling back off the track of the other dogs and the hare. She stopped several times and circled around, jumping up and down on her three legs. Then she flushed one rabbit, barked a couple of times, and went off in another direction, hopping and jump-ing and scenting. Soon she flushed another and it ran off back along the trail. Only then did Sandy Andy decide to follow the young dogs as they hived off farther away after the initial hare. Little Robert had a huge shit-eating grin on his face as he said, "Snappy, now *that* there is a rabbit dog."

Several hours later, as the shadows gathered, the dogs came back to the trucks, exhausted but happy and fulfilled as they gathered around for Little Robert's treats. Sandy Andy was far back, of course, so nobody expected her to be up with the young dogs, but after a half hour, as we relaxed, smoking and talking and drinking the last of the coffee, she hadn't returned and Little Robert was getting worried. "Something has happened to that dog," he said. "I hope she's not stuck in a trap," I offered. "No, she'd be making some kind of noise if that was the problem. We'll have to backtrack these dogs. I hope she didn't have a heart attack and die on the trail."

So calling her name and with a growing sense of foreboding we backtracked the other dogs far into the black growth. On and on we trudged, hoping against hope she was alright but getting more and more depressed when there was no sound from her and or sign of her classic three paw tracks. It was very discouraging.

Finally, we saw some lights up ahead. There was a cabin with smoke rising from the chimney. "Let's ask their dad," said Robbie, and he and Little Robert knocked on the door. I stood behind them while Zapper hung farther back and popped another Bud saying, "I'm some ready for this. This has been a thirsty day already."

When the door finally opened, two guys with yard-long, scraggly beards and as if they had never, ever had a haircut peered out. My first thought was that they looked for all the world like they had just stepped out of the movie *Deliverance*.

"What the hell you guys want?" said the older looking of the two.

"We're looking for our dog," said Little Robert. "Three legs, hard to miss." The guys turned surly. "Nope, seen nothing all afternoon," and started to close the door. But then there was a yelping inside and Robbie said, "Dad, it's Sandy Andy," and both of them pushed inside. There indeed was Sandy Andy, tied to a chair and straining to get loose. "What the hell?" exclaimed Little Robert, rushing over and picking up Sandy Andy and trying to free her. "Hey," said one of the *Deliverance* duo, "That's our dog. We found her with no collar. No tag. No nothing. She's ours now so get your ass out of here."

Just then Zapper burst into the cabin, his massive frame filling the doorway and looking like a fierce Viking warrior about to sack a monastery on an undefended island in the Irish Sea and none too pleased about the lack of gold he saw on the altar. "Hey you guys got any beer?" The older one gave him a harsh look and said, "No, we ain't got any beer. Now you take off before we get ugly." With that he started to pick up a hunting knife lying on the table.

Now Zapper was very fast for a really big guy and in a flash, he grabbed both guys by the beards and yanked their heads down hard, causing the first guy to drop the knife.

"No beer? Well that's not very neighborly of you assholes. I get some ugly when there's no beer around." He kept pulling on their beards and then letting go a little so they bobbed up and down, each time he pulled a little harder. Their faces got redder and redder and I thought Zapper might well pull their beards clean off.

By now Little Robert had Sandy Andy untied and in his arms. He'd also noticed the buckle of Sandy Andy's collar in the fireplace. "They burned her collar. They burned her collar," he exclaimed. Zapper got a furious look on his face then. "You boys are going to have to buy a new collar. Pronto."

"We don't have any money," said the smaller dude, more subdued now since Zapper held him most firmly. "No money at all. You can search the cabin."

"Well hell," said Zapper, "then we'll have to beat it out of you, or take something out in trade." By then he had their beards wrapped around both of his hands and he yanked harder as he looked around. "Well look at that gentlemen, looks like these boys have a nice sack of weed over in the corner. Snappy, you go and pick it up and take that crappy shotgun they got hanging over the fireplace along too. That'll about pay for the collar and our aggravation." Then he yanked extra hard on their beards and pulled them down onto the floor, standing over them with balled up fists as they sputtered and raged.

"And boys, don't even think about doing anything about this little mishap you just had. Now that I know where you live you best be friggin' good. Your cabin is a long, long way from any fire hydrant. Be a shame if you had even a little fire, a fine cabin like this would be burned to the ground before the fire dudes got here at all. You dubs can chalk this up to experience and call it good."

"But have some beer handy next time I come around, I always get plumb thirsty out in the woods. And I'm out and about these woods a jeasly lot of time. Meantime if you're good little boys, I'll drop the gun out by the rud. Wouldn't want you defenseless with all the varmints you got around here."

This was the longest speech we'd ever heard Zapper give and we were very impressed with the whole thing. Both *Deliverance* dudes continued to mutter and curse but remained sitting there on the floor as we headed out.

Back at the trucks, Little Robert decided to let Sandy Andy ride in the cab of his pickup while the other dogs rode in their cages in the back. "She's had a tough day," he said, feeding her some beef jerky. "Imagine what those two clowns could have done to her if we hadn't found her." "Probably try to mate with her," Zapper offered, and Little Robert shivered. "Don't even joke about it, those guys look like they could do something like that."

Zapper carefully put the bad lads' shotgun up against a tree by the end of the tote road. Robbie looked puzzled and asked, "Why did you do that?" Zapper smiled. "I want them knuckleheads to know I'm a man of my word." He paused. "Especially when it comes to playing with matches," he said as he threw down a full pack, right beside the shotgun.

Then we all headed for the general store to get some much-needed refreshment. Little Robert and Robbie took their dogs and headed out. In our truck, Zapper drove, grinning all the while. He was quite pleased with himself and grew a tad philosophical as we drove along. "My father was right again. Never grow a beard, he said, it's not an asset in a fight and it could hold you back." Then he added, "You guys take the weed, I'll get some more Buds when we stop for gas. This has been a fine day all around."

And so it was. Portland and Camden and the Cape may have become almost totally gentrified and tamed down to nothing in recent years, but the "Wild, Wild East" lives in other parts of the Pine Tree State and not just in Carolyn Chute novels neither.

Animal Control Officer

MY WIFE Sunny sent me down to mail a package and I was chatting with Little Robert the other day in the post office when Clemmie Gillespie came by to mail some letters and said hello. "The Widow," as she is known around town since moving to the old Carnegie estate ten or twelve years ago, is famous in our town of Little Harmony for being very, very nice, very, very rich and very, very large, sort of a modern Lucy Flucker Knox, wife of the Revolutionary War general who settled up by Thomaston. She is also quite famous in certain circles for claiming that Pepper Pot Johnson, the older brother of Zapper, was and is "dependable."

She's the only person ever to make such a claim, at least according to Little Robert. "The only thing dependable about that dude," said Little Robert, "is the fact that every deer he ever shot was standing within fifty yards of a road. You can depend on that." Road runner he is, Pepper once spotted a decoy buck in a field up in Bowdoinham put there by the game wardens. He then proceeded to get out and drop his pants to moon the warden's camera before getting back into his truck. He then drove away waving happily for the watching game wardens.

Now you have to understand, Pepper acting as "animal control officer" usually gunned down a few pheasants the Sunday before the opening of the bird season. He said he was doing it both for "the pot" and "to teach those dumb as a flounder pheasants some fear of the gun before the season begins." One of those early pheasants he gunned down some years back was a huge cock pheasant which had gotten up on the Widow Gillespie's lawn and in among her flower beds. Driving by in his truck, Pepper saw that pheasant and jumped out of his truck and chased it, trying to get it away from her house. He finally got the cock to fly back over the mailbox and then he fired both barrels. Bang. Bang. Said pheasant then swooned pleasantly onto the lawn.

This quite naturally caused the Widow Gillespie to come running out flapping her own hefty wings and shouting, "What's going on? What's going on?" To give Pepper his due, he may be slow on his feet, but his brain works real fast, and I'd have to say, well. As he told Zapper later, "For crumb's sake, she was in quite a state. She calmed down some though when I told her I was an animal control officer and that old pheasant was carrying the bird flu. 'Didn't want you infected and all, Ma'am,' I said. Then she was some pleased."

Amazingly, Pepper and the Widow Gillespie hit it off as a result of this incident, and from then on, his pickup was often in her dooryard all hours of the day and night. Little Robert once asked her how she liked Pepper and she replied with a warm glow. "He is a fine young man. He keeps my yard free of varmints no matter when they show up. For some reason, they seem to like the old Carnegie place and I guess I've inherited them. But Pepper is about the best animal control officer around. A lot of people tell me that and I don't think they're kidding, I think they're a little jealous he does such a good job tending to my critters."

Now before I even knew who Pepper Pot Johnson was, I used to see his somewhat scruffy lobster boat in the harbor. On the stern it had big letters spelling out "TANG." In my naïve way, I thought maybe his father or uncle had been in the navy during World War II and sailed on the *Tang*. After all, the *Tang* was quite a famous submarine. It had been going after a Japanese convoy during the war and loosed a torpedo, only to have the damn thing come around in a circle and sink the *Tang* instead. The commander of the sub ended up getting the Medal of Honor for saving his crew after the sinking, which always seemed something of a stretch to me, but then I was never swimming in the middle of the Pacific Ocean after dark either.

Later, after I got to know Pepper, I asked him about the name on his boat. He drew himself up to his true six-foot-six size and said, "It's 'cause I'm always on the lookout for righteous tang." The next time I saw Little Robert, he filled me in even more. "I know, I know." He laughed. "I once asked Pepper what was the difference between righteous tang and unrighteous tang? Pepper didn't miss a beat, he just answered, 'There ain't no such thing as unrighteous tang.'" Now Snappy, that guy can be a torment, for sure, but he was right about that, I've often thought that the worst piece of tang I ever had was"—and here Little Robert paused for maximum effect—"excellent."

Around town, Pepper's pursuit of the fair sex became legendary and a lot of guys (and gals) had a story or two to tell about Pepper. He was relentless, yes, but he was never insistent after the initial overture and he took any and all refusals with good grace. I know one time he came to our house at 11 p.m. with a full complement of coon hounds and asked if my wife Sunny wanted to go coon hunting in the moonlight.

"It's some beautiful, little darling, just like you." Sunny said no, at least in part because he had brought along some cold coon sandwiches on Wonder Bread to eat during the hunt. Being a whole grain sort of person, she didn't object to the cold coon (which is actually quite tasty with enough mayonnaise). It was the Wonder Bread, I guess, what put her off her feed and the whole expedition.

Now the annual pheasant stocking program is under much better control, with timed releases and all kinds of rules and regulations about where and when they will be let go; and maybe other places, always was. For sure rod and gun clubs often supervise things quite nicely. But during the 1970s and early 1980s in Little Harmony, it was a mass dumping of birds hither and yon, mostly yon. But it sure was a lot of fun. Back then, the state had this program whereby local farmers raised hundreds of pheasants during the summer, turning them loose a couple of days before the bird season began. In Little Harmony, it was Farmer Black who raised them and who decided where they were going. And the few nimrods he told where they were going, well they told a few others and they told a few others and so it went.

After they were released, for days there'd be hundreds of pheasants running all around a couple of big fields, seeking out the feeding trays they were used to, mumbling to themselves if hens or cackling to themselves if cocks, "Where the hell is the grub?" "Damn I'm hungry, what's going on, it's been days since he fed us."

They'd be running a bit crazily here and there, "Is it here? Is it over there?" Well, after all, they'd found precious little to eat since being "released," nothing except some bugs and some small, wild seeds. "Doesn't that taste hellish," they'd be saying. "Where is that corn?" Some of the more dim-witted (now "mentally challenged") pheasants got some hope when they saw the first pickups cruising by. "Oh good, Farmer Black is finally bring us our grub out to us. Isn't that nice? Let's go and welcome him. Look he's running toward us. Wait a minute. That's not a pail of corn . . . uh-oh."

Two days later at dawn, however, their real troubles began. It was the "Wild, Wild East."

In spades.

Crazed meat hunters, all-around layabouts wanting to show the world they were true hunters, youngsters on their first shoot, they'd all be out in full force congregating near the game laden fields. Bang. Bang. Bang-Bang, Bang-Bang. Bang-Bang. God what a slaughter it was those first few days! And of course the Sunday before was action packed as well. Eager meat hunters would ride the roads that day too, picking off a few dazed birds just to get their eye-hand coordination together and a few illegal meals in the freezer to get a jump on the season.

Some guides didn't like that pheasant situation. But others did. It was often a fine way to establish some good reputations with out of state or novice hunters you were guiding. They thought you were quite the guide when they filled their limit and saw a ton of birds. Of course, all that had to happen during the first week of the season. Most assuredly, you did not want to be taking any paying customer out pheasant hunting later in the season what with the early mass slaughter those early days, and the relentless coyotes and fox for whom Thanksgiving Day came real early. "Imagine," said more than one vixen, "what a bountiful harvest, even the ones that aren't wounded are some easy pickings."

Normally Gus wouldn't take sports out after these on these semi-tame pheasants. But he would once in a while when I really insisted. Normally he'd simply say, "Snap, you know I've shot with the Queen. This is too embarrassing." And then when I looked at him funny because I had been there too, he'd add, "Well, we were in the next glen anyway." And he simply refused to take his Britney spaniels out on peasants. "What, and ruin them for grouse? Not on your life," he'd insist indignantly.

Pheasants like to run and run before flushing, while Maine's premier game bird, the grouse, will often hold tight in thick cover and only flush as a last resort so pointing dogs can get confused and out of phase with all those manic pheasants thrashing about and cackling crazily. German shorthairs, on the other hand it is said, can make a real sport out of it.

This one opening day, however, as a special favor to me (I had to bribe him with two bottles of Glenlivet), Gus was out guiding a most rough and ready chap because I'd signed the sport up early in the summer, but then couldn't actually take him. Ralph was a nice enough guy, a tax accountant the rest of the year. He loved looking the part of outdoorsman, what with a big Mexican leather hat with a large brim and a long cock pheasant feather in the headband. "Please remove the feather," Gus said with all the dignity he could muster when he first saw it. "It is simply bad luck."

The sport complied. Most Maine Guides do have an air of authority about them, deserved or undeserved as the case may be. And Gus looks even more authoritative than most. This Ralph then brought out his Winchester 5 shot pump 12-gauge. Gus made him put in the plug to make it legal so the sport could only blast three times at one pheasant before having to reload. This is a good law, although Ralph didn't like it. "I should be able to shoot five times if I want." "Not with me," Gus answered.

Not that Gus needed to worry about the plug load in any case as matters turned out. The sport had used some kind of "not really for gun cleaning" cheap oil on his gun. It left a varnish-like residue which in turn gummed up the mechanism so that his shotgun wouldn't fire. According to Gus, pheasant after pheasant rose and presented themselves for slaughter. Some rose from behind the junipers. Some from behind the pine trees. Some from behind the apple trees. Some in front of the apple trees. Some from in front of the pine trees. Some from the short grass. Some the long grass. It was some jeesly parade, all the time, all over the fields and hollows where the pheasants had been released.

The pheasants would crackle loudly and fly up with a big whirling of wings. The sport would raise the gun and fire, only to have nothing happen. Over and over. The sport got some agitated and jumped up and down. "For crumb sakes, what the hell is wrong with this damn gun?" Several times, Gus broke the gun open and put it back together again after rubbing it madly with his handkerchief, but out in the field like that, there was no WD-40, let alone Hoppie's, to make things right.

Gus swears this happened a dozen times that morning but I can't be sure. I was stuck at home watching the half-assed crew who had come to my house pouring a cement floor in my barn. "Can't you guys come back another day?" I pleaded as I heard all the shooting from the nearby fields and roads. "Nope," said the foreman, "we got the see-ment coming today and today it is we pour."

By the time Gus came at noon, he was near true madness. "Can I borrow your old Stevens?" he pleaded, "the gd sport wants to use my Purdy this afternoon." Now Gus had the most beautiful shotgun any of us had ever seen, a glorious rose and scroll engraved side by side 16-gauge with a Beesley action from the early twentieth century.

"Gee Gus." I grinned. "I hope you wouldn't spoil your fine Purdy by using it on the big old half-wild pheasants. Debasing your firearm that way? Even thinking about it, you should be ashamed of yourself. I hope they don't hear about it at the gunsmith you took us to in Edinburgh. They learn about all those tame pheasants milling around like turkeys and they're not even the wild kind in South Dakota or Iowa either, well they'll for sure ban you for life."

"Just give me your gun," demanded Gus. "He can't hurt that damned iron pipe of yours." Now my old Stevens side by side is a 16-gauge, old but battered, with a piece of wood tacked onto the butt plate to fit the shooter's shoulder, it looks almost homemade. From 1920s, well worn, but with its simple mechanism and only two shots in two separate barrels, it is far less likely to misfire. In my time, I've missed a lot of birds and small game, but never because the old Stevens misfired.

I misfired.

Well it all ended well enough, I lent Gus my Stevens, the sport got his limit in the early afternoon and was jumping around with glee. I guess Ralph really wasn't such a bad shot once he got a gun that actually fired when you pulled the trigger. In any case, he turned out to be a very appreciative client and tipped Gus a lot more than the shoot was really worth, but he seemed very grateful to not go home empty handed after the punk-poor way the hunt started out that day. He even offered to buy the old Stevens. "That gun can some shoot," he said several times, "I'll give you $400 cash money on the barrelhead for it."

I didn't take him up on his offer, but I did reward myself for helping Gus out with my gun by sneaking away from the concrete crew for an hour to load up on a few of the critters before dusk after Gus finally brought back my gun.

Well now that I remember that total day, it actually didn't work out all that well for me. True, I did get a brace of pheasants, one cock and one hen in the waning minutes of the afternoon, but when I came back to my barn, I found the crew gone and my floor all poured. But those yahoos had left out the drain. No drain in the middle of the floor a flat concrete surface so no place for the water to run. So from then on, for every rainstorm since, for over forty years when I see standing water on my barn floor, I think of how much aggravation those two birds really cost me. I probably should have taken the sport up on his offer for my Stevens to ease my pain.

No, I'm not sad Farmer Black no longer qualifies for the state pheasant raising program. And neither is Gus.

But Pepper sure is.

Duck Feathers Destroy a Friendship

NOW I WANT to say at the outset that Big Gus was and still is probably right, that duck hunters can be the best hunters around. They follow the game laws and pick up their decoys when they get their limit, even when they're way out to sea and nobody's watching. Hell, I admire a lot of them myself. And Gus and I have had some good old boys in the blind even half in the bag who wouldn't shoot that extra duck, no matter what the temptation. That's something to be proud of—sticking to the limits when nobody is around and nobody is counting except yourself.

Like Gus, Zapper was one of those guys when it came to ducks. He might poach a deer from time to time and certainly had been known to shoot a few other four legged critters out of season, but when it came to ducks, he was strictly by the book. I can still remember that day we hunted together one cold December dawn. It was unbelievable. The conditions were truly fantastic. A real northeaster was dropping snow and howling a gale, and we were in the perfect position.

And I do mean perfect. We'd built a little blind out of dry kai early that morning on a point with two little coves on either side. At first light and with the wind raging out of the east, maybe twenty-five mph with higher gusts, and the snow coming horizontal across the face of the little blind, it couldn't be much better duck hunting than this.

Most important of all, the tide was dropping. I know there are a christly lot of theories about duck hunting and what's the right wind and the position of the decoys and all of that and some of it makes sense, but I'll tell you this, give me a dropping tide exposing the mud flats and I'll show you some good duck shooting. If there be any ducks around, that is. You can take the wind and the clouds and the skill in setting the tollers. Just have the tide dropping over prime mudflats and you'll do all right.

Well this morning on Casco Bay there was a ton of ducks around and the gale force winds kept most of the other hunting boys at home, but Zapper and I were out there purely for some fun and we surely got it. The ducks were flying and with the wind and the dropping tide and the string set just right by Zapper, they were dropping out of the sky, wings spread, open wide, coming in unmindful of anything what with the snow and howling wind and all. They'd beat into the wind, trying to drop in between the string and the blind and they'd give you a sight picture you just couldn't miss.

And we didn't. At least not very often.

It was one hell of a day. We shot damn near our limit of blacks in the first hour with some mallards thrown in and whistlers and even old squaws flinging themselves around.

The sea ducks didn't toll in much of course, but they still often flew right over the decoys wondering in all that snow who was who. Left and right in front of us they'd go.

It was prime shooting, and I know I personally never had a better overall shooting day for ducks. Normally when snow gets on the back of your decoys they don't look like ducks but more like pieces of wood with snow on them and the ducks won't toll to them at all not even a dumb, golf course mallard. But that day, all the snow coming down didn't make a bit of difference. The blacks and the mallards just flew right over, set their wings, and dropped into the middle of the snowy decoys as if to say hello and "I'm so pleased to find a nice place with good cousins feeding here like you-all in this here blizzard."

Now Zapper was not like his brother Pepper. Pepper would still be out there banging away to fill the freezer, but Zapper, well he got close to the limit and then he said, "Snap, let's make this more sporting," and out he went, turning all the decoys over. Filled them over and put their heads under the water he did.

Every last one.

But, you know, as amazing at that sounds, that didn't slow the ducks down one bit; dammed if they didn't toll right to the upside down decoys. I've honestly never seen anything like it. We shot a few more and got our limit, and then we sat for another hour just watching the ducks tumble out of the sky and into our string and marveling about how good life could really be, even if a man didn't actually deserve it.

Now on Casco Bay, in those days when it came to hunting black ducks and mallards both, there was a skinny little guy, a real runt, who thought he was king of those birds. Thought he owned them in fact. Rascal Macintosh was his name and he always was known for being damn clever when it came to ducks. He was the head of the local Ducks Unlimited and the Casco Bay Gunners Society and like organizations and everybody always wanted to be on his good side. He was in the paper all the time too, always pontificating about how to shoot ducks and all.

To be fair now, Rascal shot his limit more than most, and got his sports their limit too, even if he had to shoot a couple for them himself. He could almost always put out a set that would draw ducks no matter what the conditions. Rascal didn't really need to be jealous of anybody, he was damned good all by himself.

But Rascal himself had a couple of serious flaws. One, he *was* jealous of anyone else with a "duck" reputation, long standing or even building. And two, he was equally well known for sucking up to wardens, something which irritated a lot of other guides. I know it did me and Gus. Rascal was always flattering them and making sure he did anything he could for them. He loved to take them out duck shooting on their days off and didn't he praise their shooting (which often wasn't really that great if the truth were told). Rascal, he always made sure they got their limit so they'd tell all the sports what a great guide he was. Which, to be truthful he was, if all you judged a man by was his ducking hunting ability, then Rascal had it made.

But Rascal also had a fierce mean streak, and he always tried to knock down an up and coming guide, especially one who knew a thing or two about hunting on Casco Bay when it came to ducks. Snoopy Waldron was one such guy, he had a great personality, great hunting and guiding ability, a great gift of gab. Snoopy, he had the whole package to be guide of the year.

He also had that unteachable dimension for a successful guide, he never admitted to be licked. Snoopy would try this and he'd try that and keep at it until the sport got his money's worth.

Snoopy's only real flaw was a never-equaled fondness for baloney sandwiches, a fondness which if you examined it too closely, could curl your hair. I mean his wife Bridget was nice enough, but she couldn't cook to save her soul. Any sports who hunted with Snoopy, well they would always have to endure for grub, not only cold baloney sandwiches on Wonder Bread and a shitload of mayonnaise, but they'd also have to listen to Snoopy saying things like, "My God, have you ever tasted such good sandwiches? Bridget can cook with the best of them."

Truth be told, of course, Bridget couldn't cook at all and she would massacre, truly massacre, any wild creature Snoopy brought home. For example, instead of cooking black duck rare, she'd fry the hell out of it until the driest, toughest, gamiest, worst tasting sea duck would beat her "special" black duck in any "great chefs of the Maine coast" cook-off. Maybe that's why she stuck to baloney on extra soft white bread ("air" my wife Sunny called it) smothered in mayo when she had a choice. And probably why Snoopy gave away more game than he kept.

But Snoopy sure had a good heart, or so we all believed at the time, and he wanted more than anything to be complimented on his guiding prowess by the powers that were, including Rascal. Truth be told, Rascal was more than a little bitchy when the word got around that Snoopy's sports were getting their limit and were some pleased about it.

It even got in the local paper that Snoopy had a lot of satisfied customers and in the guiding business, nothing beats word of mouth and positive mention in the local news rag. Rascal played them publishers like a fiddle. He got great press. But the trouble was, Rascal not only wanted to be king of the hill, he wanted nobody even half way up "his" hill, and duck shooting in Casco Bay was his hill.

And in his heart, he knew that Snoopy was the real deal. When you analyzed why he was so good at it, well Snoopy just had a hell of an eye for a blind—a super eye really—and he had the sweetest little sweet spot in the whole of Casco Bay.

He'd put out a floating blind right off Two Oak Island where there was a nice long mussel bar, which on the dropping tide, shielded a nice cove of eelgrass. Snoopy had scoped it out in the summer and put a floating blind out right where the two prime spots converged.

The eider and other sea ducks would come to the mussel bar and the blacks and mallards would fly over the bar into the eelgrass bay and wasn't that some sweet shooting. Any day the ducks were flying, they would go flying over Snoopy's blind and word got around.

Big Gus and I heard about it and made no bones about asking Snoopy to take us there on his day off. He was a good-hearted son of a gun and said he'd take us.

He was some proud of the fact that we'd asked him and proud as punch to show us. We could tell he was really excited as we loaded up the boat that glorious dawn and headed out. "You boys are going to see some shooting, dontcha know, I tell you. I had some sports out off Seguin yesterday and all I could think of was how I wished they didn't want to gun only sea ducks. I sure wanted to be over in this bay. I knew I wouldn't be using it so I let Rascal take a couple of wardens out and use it yesterday. I didn't hear from Rascal last night, that's just his way, but I know he showed those boys a good time and I know he appreciates me lending him my blind."

Well it took us quite a while to get to his favorite blind, our excitement building all the while. The wind was coming onshore and there was a hell of a swell to boot and the freezing spray was coming over the gunwales and we were all cold and anxious to get set up. Although it was something of a blue bird day, with such a stiff breeze there were still a lot of ducks flying and we were pretty excited about the shooting that lay ahead.

Hence the intense, gut churning, horrible sinking feeling we all felt when we got to the floating blind. It was filled, and I mean really filled, with duck feathers. Duck feathers and duck guts—stinking, lousy duck guts—sloshing back and forth between the float timbers and even hanging on some of the cross pieces.

Not only had Rascal and the wardens had fabulous shooting, they'd plucked and cleaned the birds right there in the floating blind. What a mess. It was horrendous. It was an unheard of insult. We were amazed. And speechless.

Poor Snoopy couldn't believe it. He had tears in his eyes. "Why the hell did he do that? Why did he shit on me this way?" he asked. "I never did anything to him. We can't hunt here today, that's for sure, it's really spoiled for us. He's really pissed me off."

I was afraid Snoopy was going to tear up even more. Maybe he did. Maybe it was just the wind. I don't rightly know at this point.

Well Gus and I were some disappointed, for sure, but we knew it was Rascal's way of saying, "Boy, you ain't so high and mighty" and "I'll teach Snoopy to get all grand ideas about his station." Probably one of the wardens commented on what a super spot it was and how whoever put the blind there knew what he was going. We never found out what set him off, not that it mattered as things turned out.

I think we got madder about the situation than Snoopy though. He was just crushed and hurt. His idol had struck him to the quick. I looked at Gus and said, "This just isn't right, he's a mean son of a bitch. Somebody should kick his ass."

Snoopy hung his head. "Well guys, I guess you're right, but Rascal got me into this business and let me tag along and I've always felt I owed him something. Let's not worry about it, we'll go over to my other blind, it's just as good. The Lord says to turn the other cheek and that's just what I'm going to do. Don't worry about it, it really doesn't bother me. It probably wasn't even wardens, probably was some out of state gunners, Massachusetts gunners even. No wardens I know would make such a mess and leave it for a fellah to clean up when next he came. It must have been some other knuckleheads hunting with Rascal, not wardens."

Maybe, maybe not.

I'd like to think not.

Of course, it bothered Snoopy like hell and of course too, the other blind wasn't nearly as good, otherwise Rascal would have borrowed that one. But it still gave us pretty good shooting and we pretty much had our limit by noon. Back at Snoopy's house we went in for lunch and, per usual, endured some more baloney sandwiches on that awful Wonder Bread. "The wonder of it," Gus once said, "was that anybody bought that foul soft bread more than once." "God, these are so good Bridget," said Snoopy, "I was really down, honey, but now I feel much better. You sure know how to treat your man."

After lunch, we thanked Snoopy for a fine hunt and drove away. "Damn Gus, we should help Snoopy out and teach Rascal a lesson," I said. "Not our fight," said Gus, and I'm sure he had a point.

Now Gus is a fine man and he stuck to his principles through thick and thin and I always admired him for it. And he surely was right, it wasn't our fight. After all, Rascal hadn't done anything to us—although he certainly would have if we'd gotten uppity on his turf. Plus Gus has an abiding belief in the law and still does to this day, God bless him. And God bless America, for sure.

Still it stuck in my craw, and that's the truth. I'd learned the most important guiding lesson of all from Snoopy and that's when things are going great, don't think it's because of you and when things are going bad, try something else. Don't give up. Don't say, it's no good today and call it quits. Keep going. Get the job done. And be thankful when the hunt turns out alright and the sport is happy. There's no guarantees about any of that.

So we were some pleased when Snoopy came up to us a week or so later and said, "Well I guess there are some other people who don't like Rascal," he said. "Somebody cut his favorite blind off Whale Boat loose. It's gone. Gone clear out to sea, must be. He's been looking for two days, can't find it anywhere. I think he knows better than to ask to use one of mine again. Boy, the Lord works in mysterious ways, don't He, dontcha know?"

Gus looked funny at me and later asked, "Was that you?" "Me?" I grinned. "Me? Me? Well not alone anyway."

The truth was, Zapper never liked Rascal before I told him about the goings on, so to him, this was a God-given opportunity to help Snoopy get his message across and just deal with Rascal on general principles. Pepper doesn't like Rascal either, so he joined in just for the hell of it. Pepper thought it was such a hellishly good idea and just a fine way to have some fun. We took the *Tang* and towed that sucker of a blind out to beyond Half Way Rock, Zapper throwing his empty beer cans at any Collins buoys he saw as we went by.

Pepper too really had a ball, laughing all the way out that night. Instead of eating his usual two or three Whoopee pies, he had six of them. Gobbled them up, saying over and over, "Don't know when I've ever had more fun," he said, "let's celebrate some more and keep towing. This gd blind is going to end up in frigging Portugal."

So "The King of Ducks" ended up looking like a real jerk when he couldn't even find his own blind. "What a dork!" guys said. "How could he lose a whole blind like that? I thought he was king of the bay." Lots of people thought it served him right. Zapper heard Rascal brought some high flying sports out that first day and then had no place to put them except on some silly, godforsaken ledge. "Suckers got soaked and only got a few birds. Rascal was some pissed when they complained out loud in the Becky's Diner about the poor shooting." He laughed. "The waitresses had some fun with him. He's a lousy tipper to boot on top of everything else."

Gus shook his head. "You tell Snoopy?"

"Tell him what?" I answered, a big shit-eating grin on my face. "There was some big tides last week, Gus, fifteen feet at least. I hear a lot of folks lost gear. All over the Bay. Rascal must not have used enough chain."

"Well, I heard the anchors was gone as well," he replied, "and I hear the wardens are on the warpath, looking for those anchors, seems Rascal has his brand welded on them." "Well," I allowed, "*I* hear the water to the west off Half Way Rock is 150 feet deep or more. I'll wish those boys some luck, but I think they'll need more than luck to find anything smaller than a sub or a World War II plane out there."

"No, I guess this will end up what folks call a real puzzlement," I added. "I'll bet Snoopy feels good about things though." I chuckled none too quietly.

Gus allowed as how he would. "Snoopy already thinks this was all the Lord's work. I wonder if he thinks those jeesly baloney sandwiches are the Lord's work too."

"That I could not say, Gus, that I could not say." I grinned.

An Uncommon Double

"**T**HE KID'S** a great wing shot, dontcha know, you have to give him that," Pepper was expounding one fine fall Saturday morning at the recycling center which had naturally replaced the old dump as a common ground meeting place in our town. "If he wasn't such a good shot, this wouldn't have happened."

It was the day after Pepper's youngest, Tad, aka "Tadpole" had been fined by Judge Alvin "Angry" Swenson for shooting a crow out of season. Poor Tadpole got his nickname from his own father. "Sometimes he's as numb as the butt-end of a tadpole," his father once said when the kid was in the third grade and the name stuck. In a small town like Little Harmony, you want to be some careful about what you call your kid in public.

Now eighteen, tall and lanky and working as his father's stern man, Tadpole was a very likable young man, actually very water savvy and dependable. A good urchin and scallop diver as well, he was damn loyal too to his father. Last year when Pepper had some territorial disputes with the Collins boys, a big clan of sometime but still big time bullies, Tadpole and a friend had gone out in a very thick night fog, a dungeon fog as it's known in Little Harmony, and cut forty-two of the Collinses' traps. He and his buddy, Gil Largay, never told Pepper, just went out and did it. So when the Marine Patrol officer, Pappy Smenton, came by the next day to accuse Pepper, he didn't even know about the doings and had the perfect excuse, he had been at a night Red Sox game with the Widow Gillespie's church group. I know, Pepper with a church group sounds like a stretch but the Widow invited him to go with her church group and he said, "What the hell, why not?" That worked out some good. Tadpole hadn't even told him afterwards about it so Pepper, himself, was dumbfounded when the warden confronted him.

"Serves those Collins boys right," Pepper had said indignantly when he recovered from the very pleasant news. "You know they're always cutting and moving and causing havoc whenever they can. There's a lot of gear lost to those boys. Could have been any number of the lads getting even, not that you ever could get totally even with those hammer heads."

The Marine Patrol officer nodded. "I know. I know, Pepper. I'd like to put those friggin' malcontents away for good, you guys know that, but you can't go cutting their traps like that just cause they do. So you tell whoever did it to stop doing it. I won't have a war on my watch, I'll put all of you in jail first."

Now Pepper was very proud of his boy when he learned the full story, and wished he hadn't labeled him "Tadpole," but of course by then it was way too late. As for his exploits late at night out on the foggy water, doing battle on behalf of his dad, Tadpole allowed later as how the thrill and the excitement and sense of accomplishment "was better than sex, at least the kind of sex I'm able to get at the present time. My dad says the sex will get better though."

But back to the Tadpole and his run-in with the law, I stayed around the recycling center to listen to the rest of the story. That was pretty easy to do. Pepper would start all over again as soon as someone new showed up to dump their stuff, so I just sorted the trash and waited until I heard "Tadpole is a damn fine wing shot, that's all I know." Then I tuned in again. It seems Tadpole and his friend—oddly enough Will Collins, a young member of the very clan we spoke of earlier—were out duck hunting in Quahog Bay when the incident happened.

Will had been in Vietnam and was home now for good and trying to relax. He'd been in the Marines and not just any old Marine unit. He'd done two tours in a Marine Long Range Recon team that spent a lot of time being inserted into North Vietnam for weeks at a time. It was about as dangerous a job as you could have in that war and the kid came through unscratched which added some irony to this day's events.

The only time Will came close to getting hurt was one time when a water buffalo pushed over the helo that had come to pick them up after two weeks in the NV bush. "One of the rotors came off and missed me by a hair" was all Will would say about the incident except to add, "We were some glad when the backup helo came and got us. We did dust that gd buffalo on the way out though."

So Will and Tadpole were out on Elm Island in a nice cove blind one beautiful blue bird day. The shooting was poor, just punk, only an occasional sea duck peered into the cove to look at all those black and mallard decoys, then flew away uninterested. Will did shoot one little dipper duck, a buffle-head, but that was about all so the boys were some antsy.

"Finally a big old black back gull comes in and looks over the tollers," Pepper continued. "Now I know he shouldn't have, but Tadpole jumped up and plugged that black back. Hit him solid, but on he flew, almost as if nothing had happened except the gull started a slow, slow descent into the water. Just cleared the trees on the point and splashed down in the next cove. Tadpole and Will started laughing and said. 'Too bad nobody's in that cove to see. They'd been some surprised.'

"Now how were the boys to know two Marine Patrol Officers were hunting in that next cove? Surely that was piss poor luck," said Pepper. "The wardens told the judge they were just having a bite to eat when they heard the shot and over their left shoulders came that gull, heading right into their string and then it plopped down, dead as a doornail in the middle of it.

"Well, they were some perturbed, to say the least. I guess they took it all personal like and all about them and an insult to the warden service and so on. Enraged, the two of them came boiling out of their blind and they went up over the little ridge separating the two coves. Stumbling and cursing and churning. That's when things really all went to hell.

"Will and Tadpole were laughing and high fiving at the dusting of that big black back gull when what appeared then but a huge crow. Now that sucker was flying a lot higher than the gull had been and he obviously had his eye on the falling gull, no doubt thinking, 'Well that's a gift from the gods for sure. That gull is looking damn peak-ed, I'm going to a fine meal before the other crows show up.'

"So that is probably the reason the crow wasn't paying as much attention right below him as he should have and forgot to check out the two hunters in the blind. Life's like that sometimes, but usually during the mating season. As you well know, Snappy," Pepper added.

"'That would be a hell of a shot,' Will had said, looking up at the crow and then at Tadpole. 'Let's see you hit that. That sucker is a mile up. A mile up and then some.' Well, Tadpole got a big grin on this face and standing there with one barrel still smoldering commenced to let loose with the other one. Dang it if he didn't hit that crow square and it just cleared the point before it too cratered into the next cove.

"'How's that for a double,' Tadpole yelped, 'how's that for a fine fricken' double on this do-nothing day? Two birds and not even the same kind, either. A gull and a crow in a double. That's something. I don't think anybody's ever done that around here at least.'

"That's where the bad luck came in. Even Judge Swenson admitted that to me. Angry told me, 'Pepper, that boy of yours would have beaten the gull charge, but there were witnesses to the crow. Two of them. Both wardens saw him take the shot. Now, Pepper, you know I get riled up when my court gets all clogged up with these fish and game malfractions and that damn younger fella warden, why he brings more than his fair share to my court. I've told you I get some weary of it all, but these guys had your boy dead to rights. They did say it was a hell of a shot but still, right in front of them all and the dead body dumped right into their string. For crumb's sake, Pepper, you have to admit it, there was real provocation there.

"'But I know you want to be proud of your boy and I think you should be,' Angry continued, 'although it would be better for all of us if you two obeyed more than a couple of the game laws around here. But whenever I've seen your boy before, you've been spouting off on something and sopping up all the atmosphere so I've never heard the poor kid talk on his own. But I think he's got a good head on his shoulders. Stood right there in open court and told his story.

"'Your honor,' he said, very respectfully. 'I would never shoot a crow. They be nature's undertakers and without them who would clean up all the road kill around here? So no sir, I wouldn't go shooting them for sport. It was pure reflex. You see I had just fired to scare off a black back gull, he was diving down to get the little tender dipper Will had shot earlier and was drifting to shore, coming in to carry it off dontcha know. You know how sad it is when those black backs feast on the little eider ducks in the spring. Them little eiders are nothing but some fine sushi to those big mean black backs. So I tried to scare him off. I'm super sorry about the crow though, I got confused, thought it was another black back. Tried to scare him off too, for sure.'

"Angry continued to recount Tadpole's story. 'Judge, I didn't think I would hit him. Not with him at that altitude. No sir. Not at all. I didn't think anybody could of hit him. I was the most surprised of all when I seen him heading down. I first thought he was just scaling down into those tall pines on the shore. I had no idea he would come a calling on those wardens. No sir. And I'm real sorry about what happened to Will. I feel like it was my fault. Spend all that time in Nam and never get hurt and then I take him duck shooting in the bay and this happens.'"

"'I did feel bad for the Collins kid,' added the judge. 'The kid took a hell of a digger that day.' Poor Will had gotten so rattled by the wardens showing up like that, he bounded over a couple of seaweed covered rocks running toward them, slipped and hit his head and broke his ankle in two places. The wardens had to carry him over to his boat and because of his head injury, alert the EMTs and hang around until they came. Bet they enjoyed that. But imagine doing terrible two tours in Vietnam and never get injured and then to be home relaxing and break your bones. Sad story. 'Will's a good lad and he served his country, he didn't need this aggravation, no he didn't. You understand, Pepper, if he'd been the one, I'd let him off.'"

"Judge Swenson continued and grinned at me, which of course for him was more like a grimace, but you got the message. 'I think your boy told me the best improvised story I've heard since you conned me with that story about your brother and his mail order bride.'

"Well, I said, Judge, I've know you for a long time and I've even appeared in front of you're a few times, although with more positive results now that I think about it. But I'd have to say this is a pretty open and shut case and you did just what you had to do. I do appreciate you fining the boy only $100. I lent him the money to pay the fine so now he can chop the wood for the winter to repay that loan, so it won't all be bad, at least for me."

Nobody ever said Pepper wasn't philosophical.

And his own proud history with Angry Swenson was pretty much a hoot too. Back after the Korean War, Pepper's older brother Ivor had ordered himself a mail order bride from Korea and he'd gone over to pick her up (or out, I'm not totally clear). He was gone for a couple of weeks as there was a snag in the paperwork once he got there—or he tried out another bride and that took a bit longer. Anyway, when Pepper, Zapper, and Ivor's father Halvor was alive, he was some kind of fierce highliner. He fished from one end of this long island to the other, on both sides of the channel and you never, ever set in those waters least you wanted to lose all your gear and possibly your life.

Now there's something of an unwritten code among lobstermen, at least the highliners. Some dub or mouthy youngster drops a few traps in their territory and they won't cut their buoys first off. They might drag the interlopers traps a far piece first. If there is a next time, well then they might tie off the buoy so he can only find it on a low drain. If it persists, they might haul a few of his string and put a lot of big rocks or bricks with obscenities on them inside the traps.

And Zapper came up with a corker on his own. A couple of new boys began edging into his territory from the south. Zapper skipped a few steps and tied beer bottles to their warp line about thirty feet down so when the bottle came up and hit the hauler, it exploded in a shower of glass all over the deck. Scared the piss out of them and messed up their deck some good. And the young lads then had to worry about every other trap had to haul that day. They got the idea and moved out of the area on the very next set.

So the whole idea on the coast is to save the cutting for last, or next to last. Last is fisticuffs or a shot fired across the bow of the offender. That's the last resort.

But Halvor Johnson was one old-timer who had no patience for interlopers, none at all. And no patience for the slow moving code of the highliners, although he was as big a highliner as you can get. No, Halvor he skipped a lot of steps when he got aggravated.

I remember one day the old man he found a guy fishing his territory for the first time, just right there big as life hauling his traps like he belonged there in Halvor's territory. Well sir, Halvor just unlimbered his rifle and wanged off a few 30-30 rounds across the bow of the interloper. No warning. No threats. Nope, just a couple of rounds. Now this young guy was younger, bigger and stronger than Halvor, but not dumb, and once he got over his shock, he came to pronto and waved frantically and yelled smartly, "Sorry, sorry Halvor, I'm super sorry, but with that tide running so strong, a few of my traps went walking, won't happen again."

And it didn't.

So, there was this prime fishing ground controlled by Halvor and when he was dying, he called all his boys together and with a map of the area, he drew firm red lines.

"After you boys put me in the ground and grieve some with your poor mother who will miss me more than most, Pepper, you fish north of the bridge. Ivor, you fish south of the bridge both sides and Zapper, you being a carpenter and all you don't need much territory; you fish between our landing and Whistler Cove, but only on the west shore." Then he died.

The boys honored Halvor's wishes for a couple of years, although every season, Zapper would put in a few more traps on the other side of the channel and creep into his two brothers' territory. But since he never fished more than thirty or forty traps all told, they let him be. He was kin after all, although that wouldn't have prevented serious retaliation if he'd gone to say one hundred traps. No, they'd have cut him ahead of just about anybody else then.

But when Ivor went to Korea for that long stretch, Pepper couldn't resist. He saw his main chance and he acted on it. Fast. He brought a hundred traps into Ivor's territory the first day and another hundred the second and by the third, he was still hankering for all of Ivor's missed catch. Working late like that, he kind of lost track of time or so he said, and he acted real surprised when the warden came upon him hauling at ten o'clock at night.

Now my wife Sunny likes art and she's dragged me to museums more than once. I try to focus on real scenes and I've always liked paintings of sea life. You know that fellow Wyeth's painting of the guy hauling a lobster trap at night, all glowing with phosphorous and the hauler looking like an out and out villain.

Well that didn't do Pepper in, that kind of thing; no, it was the fact that he was singing and laughing and eating some of those Whoopie pies he likes so much, and the warden heard him from a mile away. Pepper was so excited at getting all of Ivor's lobsters, he couldn't contain himself. Well caught he was, fair and square and the warden knew he had an open and shut case. He had witnessed the late hauling and he got the case brought before Angry Swenson, who was well known for throwing the book at miscreants, really hitting them hard.

So we all thought Pepper was done for that time. He'd lose his license for sure. True, he hadn't been pulling other people's traps at night, but he had been pulling his own and that, in the eyes of the law, is almost as bad. Plus the warden had him dead to rights. But there was another side to Judge Swenson, why no lawyer or prosecutor really was comfortable practicing in his courtroom even though they liked the way he'd bash and mash miscreants if he felt like it.

Angry was a tyrant for sure, but more importantly from their point of view, he was erratic as hell. Angry never paid a lot of attention to precedent or the law books, some wags said. No, he went by the seat of his pants a lot of the time and that worked out in Pepper's favor because Angry Swenson liked to be amused. He found most law work boring and he liked drama in the court to break things up.

And Pepper, he was always good theater. He stood in front of the judge, head bowed, all dressed up in his Sunday go-to-meeting suit. Shaking his head slowly from side to side when Angry asked him what was he thinking. "I lost my head Judge, I plumb lost it. You know my older brother Ivor, he's a good fellow and all, but he's always lorded it over me and our other brothers, claiming he's our daddy's only own true son and when he went off to Korea to get his wife, well it was too good an opportunity to get back at him for all those years of lording it over me. He had it coming, dontcha know.

"Your Honor, try as I might," Pepper continued, "I just could never find favor with my pappy, just couldn't stand up tall in his eyes and I thought, you know, my pa, dead these many years now, well, he would want me to show my true colors and be a man about it and catch every christly lobster I could. That's the code he lived by and even, sir, died by if I may say so. His last thoughts on earth were about lobsters I know that, Your Honor and about dividing up his territory in that righteous way as he checked out because that was what was important to him. I was thinking of him you see. Wanting to stand tall in his eyes and showing him, lobsters is all I really ever thought of or cared about too. I've always wanted him to know I wanted to be a highliner just like him for jeesly sakes. I'm sorry Your Honor, plumb sorry, I just was trying to look some good in the eyes of my dearly departed pap who I loved so much."

Well by now Warden Holton is rolling his eyes and his head both and the prosecutor is laughing, not out loud, of course, that would anger the judge, but he's got his head down in his briefcase as if looking for a lost winning Lotto ticket and thinking he sees it. Cause they both know Old Man Johnson beat the crap out of Pepper and Zapper too, although not

Ivor, and Pepper was fond of saying the happiest day of his life was the first time he tasted true tang and the second happiest was the day his son of a bitch of a father died.

By now even Judge Swenson is having a hard time keeping a straight face and he knew it wouldn't be good for his reputation if he started laughing like a lunatic, which is really what he felt like doing at that moment. So right then he jumps up from the bench and says, "I can't take away a man's livelihood. It wouldn't be right. Case dismissed."

Now that stopped the warden's suppressed laughter dead cold for sure. And the prosecutor? Well, he whipped his head out of the briefcase so fast, he whacked it some good on the bottom of the table and he ended up letting out a low moan.

Even Pepper was speechless, but he regained his composure ahead of the others as he bowed his head again and said, "I thank you for justice, Your Honor. I thank you for true justice and I know my old pappy does too. I just pray I can do right by him fishing strictly in the daytime from now on. But thanks to you Judge, I am going to try to do just that. I want to make you and him proud. Both of you."

By then Angry Swenson, of course, was out of the courtroom and on his way to his first martini of the night, although certainly not of that day.

Big Gus Saves
a Young Girl

I **AM FORTUNATE** to have three wonderful grandchildren. One boy, Dusty, is a true child of Maine, living in a house with a wood stove and living on the edge of the "Wild, Wild East." At five he's already into tracks and birds and getting wild oysters when we're out on the flats. Probably because he lives it, he doesn't ask too many questions about my life as a Maine Guide unless I bribe him with a Classic Coke, which he is not allowed to guzzle at home.

Steve, on the other hand, lives in a big city so whenever he comes to Maine, he always has a lot of questions. He once did a report to his suburban Washington school on the nine wild turkeys he saw on his visit to Maine. Of course, none of the kids in the school had ever seen one, let alone nine so they didn't believe him although the teacher tried to validate his claims.

Interestingly, like so many other suburban children he's seen a ton of deer, even ones eating his mom's flowers, so that part of the Wild, Wild East seems pretty passé to him. And so he truly feels sorry for the people who live in northern and eastern Maine and have a hard time even getting a doe permit, let alone getting a doe.

His older brother, Mikey Roach, on the other hand has no interest in the out of doors and only loves sports and chess, not the wilderness. He is a fine lad, just not interested in hunting and fishing stories. Mikey would rather be on the court or in the world of Dungeons and Dragons or playing in a chess tournament.

Anyway, one day at Christmas, Steve asked me what was the best game to eat and I did give him my unvarnished reactions. "Bear tastes a lot like sirloin steak fat, delicious but very rich, you couldn't eat much of it without feeling sick." His eyes got big as saucers. "You ate a bear? Yuk!" Unfazed, I carried on. "And moose, well moose can be real dry or taste like pine needles depending on what it's been eating, but mostly it doesn't have much of a taste on its own, but it goes great with anything. '

Now our kids were brought up on "moose burgers" and "moose-getty" but we always had to add a lot of fat to the meat to make it tasty or make sure it absorbed a nice sauce to give it real flavor. "What about deer?" he asked. "Well to me venison has a very distinctive flavor, and if I got to eat wild meat every week, it would be venison, as long as your grandmother Sunny didn't overcook it.

"But really, the best tasting wild meat I've ever had was sora rail. That is a taste masterpiece, a tiny speck but a masterpiece nevertheless. Yes sir, I'd make it rail and rice any day of the week, for sure."

Like most people, even most hunters here in Maine, Steve had no idea what I was talking about. Unfortunately, we didn't have any rail in the freezer to show Steve and let him taste some, but his question did remind me of one of my favorite Big Gus stories.

It was Big Gus who discovered rails in Merrymeeting Bay and showed me how to hunt those fantastic little game birds, rails, both sora and Virginia. Not many Maine Guides do rail shooting, but Gus is one and he's a real master of it. For my money, Big Gus more or less put rail shooting on the Maine map. Now rails migrate like other wildfowl and they really congregate in Merrymeeting Bay in the early fall before they head south. They fatten up on its wild rice for the long flight south because I think they end up in South America or some far-away place.

The rails are drawn to the acres and acres of wild rice which grows thick and abundant among the reeds of Merrymeeting Bay. They are pretty, small, green and yellow birds which make a distinctive chirping sound. Soras and Virginias hide in the wild rice and reeds and to make them flush, you have to use a canoe or kayak and go into the middle of the big expanses of wild rice.

It is a lot of work poling or pushing your canoe through the heavy rice and reeds. And it has another big drawback, you can really only do it at high tide. The very top of the tide is best because those reed and wild rice tangles are impenetrable most of the time. So the timing of your hunt is very important. You need to get in and out and not get trapped in the thick reeds when the tide drops.

Now when you flush them, rails kind of jump up and fly a little way before settling back into the five- or six-foot high wild rice. Because they are so small, you only use a very light shotgun like a .20-gauge with # 8 shot and you have to shoot them at the right distance otherwise you get a lot of lead (now steel) in your food. But the bag limit was twenty-five in those days (and still is today I think), so you could theoretically get a lot of action although in practice a bag total of half that per gun on one tide is pretty good.

Rails, sora or Virginia, are well worth hunting for eating purposes, even though it might take eight or ten to make a meal. Big Gus is a real genius when it comes to getting a canoe down the little waterways and he delights in taking sports there although it does take a certain, special kind of sport to enjoy the hunt. I always loved going with him, sitting in the bow of the canoe and acting like the sport.

For me, the shooting of the rails is really secondary to having an excuse to be out on Merrymeeting Bay in early September. The duck hunting season hasn't begun yet so there are hundreds—and on some days, thousands—of blue and green wing teal, the first of the ducks to head south. And no hunters. Now for my money, green or blue teal are the perfect duck. They decoy very well, die relatively easy compared to the thicker downed black ducks or mallard and are the best tasting wildfowl I know save the rails.

When you go into the reeds you are focusing on the rails, but the clouds of teal off in the near distance, wheeling around, their blue and green wing bars flashing iridescent in the sun, are really a magnificent sight. And we often just stop and watch them. Even the most hard-hearted sport is excited by the sight, and unless severely restrained, want to take a shot at them under the guise of "there was a rail somewhere underneath that flock." The Bay must have looked this good or even better back in Indian days.

Also, game wardens are very protective of Merrymeeting at all times and especially during the run up to the duck season, and they are very likely to swarm around when they hear your first shots, thinking that some dim wit is jumping the duck season.

It was always fun to watch them come racing out the first time on a glorious early September day we were out on the Bay. They always seem disappointed they can't arrest you so it's sometimes it's a nuisance to have them barreling over like that but, as this story will tell you, sometimes it is very good that they come out to investigate.

So among the local guides, Big Gus owns the bay for rail, no question about it. His green canoe is a fixture in early September and there are some dedicated rail hunters who come just to be there every fall. As I've said more than once, Gus is a real gentleman hunter, a strict observer of bag limits, end and start of hunting times, and also quite elegant.

He also has eleven different sizes and types of L.L.Bean boots and he's very, very particular about which one to wear with what conditions. "Snappy, we've got three inches of wet snow, go with these." Gus is the only hunter in Maine that I know about who often hunts with a Purdy shotgun although when he is rail shooting, he often uses his classy little Parker.

That was a good thing he did, that September when he saved the young girl's life. The Parker may or may not have had something to do with it, I told Steve. Gus's sport was something out of a picture book, a cute little thing with red hair and a dusting of freckles and at fourteen or so, blissfully unaware of boys and proms and pom poms.

Big Gus called her "that little slip of a girl" or "that bonnie lassie," but she was quite the dedicated hunter, or huntress to be more precise. She was a hell of a shot too, was Julie McTavish. Gus took her out to the skeet range once and she hit twenty-three out of twenty-five clays and wasn't even winded. Julie McIntosh was impressive in general and Gus, in particular, was truly impressed with on many levels, one being she was half or even one third the size of his own wife, the famous Willimina Sessions.

This was not easy to do. I mean impressing Gus unless you were an English lord or duke, has always been plumb hard to do. And as for the distaff side, he'd already found a wife who was perfect for him, although he could become a bit wistful when speaking about Julie. Willimina was a fine specimen for sure: 220 pounds, dry. All muscle. Big head with lots of brain cells and a palpable lust for Gus. A real two fisted drinker, she liked to shoot submachine guns on FBI ranges which is where they met. She owns and operates a modified Armalite AR-15 courtesy of Bushmaster. But more of that gun toting side of her later.

And in Gus's mind, you could not, would not, never ever, do better than Willimina. "I was put on this earth for her," he said more than once. "She is just a damn fine woman all around." Now when Pepper first heard about their joint firing of submachine guns on the range, however, he was flabbergasted. "Sum bitch, I didn't even think they let women near that kind of weapon. This could be bad for a lot of us."

But there was something about the distaff side of our species which has often been attracted to Gus's mature aloofness. He once taught a course at the local community college on the environment and utilizing its resources or some such topic and his classes were chuck full, all the time, every semester when he taught it. How he ever got "The Politics of Environmental Change" into the curriculum I'll never know.

Gus always tried to bring students out into nature and expose them to its realities. We kidded him about using them to drive deer to where he could shoot them, but that was only us having some fun.

Once two young lasses, overcome with Gus in the classroom, or perhaps the idea of him out of the classroom on a remote backcountry ridge or isolated island, begged him to take them duck hunting. He reluctantly agreed, but "Big G" as she was known in the trade and her friend Bitsa showed up in his dooryard the day he was taking them duck hunting in nylons and short skirts. I kid you not. That and lipstick too. Gus was not impressed. "I spent the whole morning keeping a fire going in the blind. I've never done that before and I don't plan to ever do it again."

But Julie was different. Julie loved the out of doors with a fierce passion and she didn't want any nonsense about being a girl. She just wanted to be out there and dressing and acting like a Maine woods woman, no frills, no nonsense, no special treatment and she got some mad if you cut her any slack.

Luckily Julie had a father who could well indulge her passion for the out of doors. He'd taken her mule deer hunting in Montana and duck shooting in Sonora. "Mr. Gus, it was wonderful shooting, hundreds and hundreds of ducks, canvas backs, widgeon, pintails, a whole array of ducks we don't see much of around here. I don't think they had any bag limits there either," she said. "They let me shoot as many as I wanted but I stopped at six though." Gus was both pleased and impressed. "This younger generation ain't all bad," he said.

Julie's idol was Debra Plowman, Maine's first female game warden who was also the first in the United States and later she became Head of the Maine Warden Service, also a first. "She's something else," said Julie. "I want to be a pioneer just like her." Gus and I had to admit you couldn't do better than wanting to be like Debra. She was a legend and deservedly so. Imagine the crap she had to take to become the first female game warden in Maine let alone the U.S. of A.

Anyway, this glorious early September day, Big Gus took Julie out on the Bay and she was shooting great guns. "She had four or five doubles and only missed once or twice. It was so much fun to watch her shoot and her excitement was contagious. That's what got me into trouble," Gus opined. "The tide started dropping fast and we were right in the middle of the rice fields so it was getting harder and harder to pole. I pushed the canoe into the thick of it and two rails came up right in front of the canoe. One broke right and one left. Julie nailed the first one to the left and then swung onto the other one. It started to fly low so she stood up to get a better shot. That's when the canoe hit a real dense patch and I tried to pole us through it."

The physics was plumb against them, for sure. Julie was leaning right to shoot and Gus was pushing hard left to free them from the tangle. When the canoe started to tip, Gus took the pole and swung it hard to the right to steady things down, but caught Julie alongside the shoulder.

Bad move.

The canoe started to tip over and the pole kept moving. It hit Julie in the head next and knocked her out. Then everybody and everything, big and small, got dumped into the water. Now the water was only six or seven feet deep but it was very murky and brown. Julie went face down and the canoe fell on top of her. Both shotguns, Big Gus's Parker and her little Browning, fell into the water.

Now I know Gus pretty well and I'm morally certain his first thought was not for Julie but for the Parker. But Gus's Maine Guide sense of priorities and his fondness for that Scottish lass both kicked in then and he swam over to her. Somehow Gus got her head up out of the water. Meanwhile the tide was going fast and pulled them out toward the middle of the Bay. By the time Big Gus got her revived, the two of them were thirty or forty yards away from where they'd spilled into the water. Luckily the canoe floated with them and they finally came to a place out of the channel where the two of them could stand up and get the canoe back upright.

Now if Gus has a weakness, it's not sex or alcohol but rather care of his feet. He is hooked, as they say, on that. Gus simply cannot abide getting his feet wet. He will do anything to keep them dry. Anything. To me, half the fun of being out in the woods is to get your feet wet, after all the Indians did this whole scene with moccasins so you know they were wet all the time, even when it was freezing and we Guides sure pretend we were—or at least could have been—them old time Indians a lot of the time. They are our heroes even though we probably wouldn't last more than a couple of days in their moccasins.

So there Gus was, in the middle of Merrymeeting Bay in September, the sun was shining and he'd saved Julie alright, but now he was soaking wet and not just his feet either. He somehow managed to get her back in the canoe and with her balancing the craft with the pole, he got himself in too, no small task for sure. To this day, I really don't know how they did it.

"Can we go back and get my gun, Mr. Gus?" Julie asked. He nodded. "We sure can Julie, we surely can." But that was easier said than done because once the tide dropped, the rice fields became an impenetrable thicket what with the reeds and the mud and all that growth and no real way to get inside the mess and back to where the canoe went over.

Gus's first thought was to take care of Julie so he got her into his Land Rover and he drove to the general store and called her father to say she was alright and then he rang up Tad Johnson. Now Gus never called Tad Tadpole, ever, so maybe that's why Tad who had been hauling traps with his dad since 5 a.m. dropped everything and rushed up to Merrymeeting Bay that afternoon to help Gus retrieve those shotguns.

"But I knew, Snappy," Tadpole said later when I asked him about it, "I knew as soon as I seen that water we were done for the day. That water is just like black coffee and skin-diving in it was some pointless. But I didn't want to let Gus down so I showed up. By the time we got things organized, it was too low to do any swimming, let alone diving in those jeesly reeds. I told him we had to call it quits for the night. Nobody would or could and certainly won't find those guns tonight, I said, and we'll be back first light, but we need some high water to get up in where you lost them."

The next day, Gus had us all there bright and early with the tide coming. We had a couple of canoes and a johnboat and Gus brought us back to where he thought they'd been when the canoe went over. The water was no clearer, nor did I expect it to be. "Gus," I said, "we'll just have to let the water drop and feel our way through things. We'll have to let our feet find those guns, our eyes will never get the job done."

Luckily, two wardens came over to help. They'd gotten a big kick out of Tadpole's earlier run-in with the coastal warden when they'd heard about it and asked him to tell them about it all over again. There's some rivalry between the inland wardens and the guys on the Marine side they call "Clam Watchers," so they like it when the coastal wardens have any problems. Ray Sader, the older of the two let out some real guffaws when Tadpole told the story all over again, "Can you imagine the look on those two dudes faces when first the gull dropped into their string and then a crow. They must have thought it was the end of the world, or you guys was ganging up on them."

The wardens especially didn't have anything good to say about the lead Sea and Shore guy, Johnnie Holton. "We call that piss-ant Yankee, 'No Slack,'" said Hank Roberts. "He'd bust his own mother for five undersized clams in a bushel, swear to Christ and he doesn't like any of your family for sure, not at all. Not even a little bit."

Jake Struthers, the other game warden, continued, "Now you want to put the bad guys away, that's for sure but you have to cut guys some slack so you can concentrate on the big deals. Boy, I'd sure like to have been there to see all that action and them having to lug Willie all the way across the island to your boat and then have to wait around for the EMTs. What a hoot."

Well Gus finally put a stop to the gabbing when he said, "Guys, the tide's dropping, I don't want my gun in the mud another night." We all grinned and got back to searching.

Tadpole got us all organized and we all got into the water. Despite all that was at stake, Gus was somewhat, no astonishingly, reluctant to get into that mud and start trooping around in it. I could see he didn't want to get his super good L.L.Bean boots ("L.L. wore these when he was high stepping") into that awful mud, so he took off his boots and jumped in with the rest of us wearing only his socks. What a sight, we were all treading around in that mud like we were going for quahogs, reaching out with our feet and toes to try to find those lost guns.

That's when we learned something new about Big Gus. He was, as I've already said, known far and wide as someone who didn't like to get his feet wet. Well this day we all now discovered he really didn't like to step on eels either. Didn't he jump nearly clean out of the water and let out a war hoop when he stepped on the first one. "What the hell was that?" he asked incredulously.

"Well it's either an eel or a snake," said Jake, cackling like a maniac. "If it's a snake, I don't think it's poisonous, the last poisonous snake in Maine was 1830 or thereabouts."

"I don't like either one of those critters," said Gus haughtily. "Snake or eel. Besides, who knows what's in the Cathance River nowadays. There could be some pet snakes let loose in that waterway. Could be an Anaconda for all I know. I don't like this situation one bit."

Now Gus didn't want to look bad in our eyes so he persisted, but he wasn't real happy about stepping on odd creatures in the muck and mud. The eels must have been attracted to his socks, that's all I can say. Gus must have stepped on three or four in the first half hour.

Luckily, his agony ended in the second half hour of trampling around in that rice and reed mess. It was one of the wardens who finally found the first gun, by stepping on it. Jake held it up triumphantly. Wasn't Gus some relieved when he gave out a big whoop and held up the Parker. Next, Tadpole got Julie's gun which was only about twenty feet away and that part of the saga ended happily.

Back at the landing, we were standing around chatting and Gus had lit up his pipe. That's when Jake congratulated Gus on making the choice to save the girl rather than the Parker first. "That took some real courage to make the right call about which of them to save. You did real good."

Then Gus got a real funny look on his face. He was never comfortable when people paid him compliments and he was painfully honest, especially about himself. He puffed on his pipe for a while before speaking, his brow all knit up with concentration.

"Well," he allowed. "I am happy I made the right call and did the right thing when I did. Julie deserved the best. Anyone of you would have done the same I'm pretty sure. I'm just glad it wasn't my Purdy going over the side. That would have made it a much tougher choice."

We never told Julie about that of course. Everybody needs a hero, even a "little slip of a girl" who could shoot gangbusters no matter who she was gunning with.

chapter
seven

Moose under Water

PETE PETERSEN, a Vietnam veteran, was, as Gus was fond of saying both before and after the hunt, "One of those guys who makes guiding worthwhile." A 1st Cavalry helicopter gunner, Pete had been wounded in both legs and the back during the 1965 fighting in the A Shau Valley. After his service, Pete taught social studies in Rumford, and against the odds, got a permit in the first Maine moose lottery in 1980.

He drew the area around Lobster Lake up in Piscataquis County where Gus had fished a lot over the years. When he won, Pete immediately called Gus whom he'd put down as his sub-permittee and now wanted to be his guide. Pete was so excited. "You've got to help me, Gus, this is the chance of a lifetime."

I agreed to help Gus but we told Peter that neither of us had shot a moose before but we'd go with him anyway and do our best to help him find the critters. "They're pretty thick up there," Gus allowed. "I'm not promising anything, Pete, but we should be able to get you on one. At least as long as you don't have to have one of those huge old bulls. I've seen a lot of cows and small bulls in that area, but then nobody was hunting them at the time. It makes a big difference when a lot of yahoos are blasting away at them."

"Nope," said Pete, "I don't want a big bull. I want a yearling bull or a young cow, I want a good eating critter. I don't care about horns or size. In fact, I just want a nice young one. The only other thing is I don't want to shoot one of the moose standing by the road. I want to really get into the bush and hunt one up. I want to really hunt it, not just road run it. That's why I'm coming to you, Gus. I know you'll do it right."

Pepper just laughed when we told him of our plans. "Of all the christly bad ideas, that one beats all. You need to drive the roads with a winch and a nice long cable and when you see a cow, pop her and winch her right out to the truck. Don't be messing about deep in the woods with a big moose. You'll get a heart attack."

Some wags had previously reckoned that the life expectancy of a moose in Little Harmony was about twenty-four hours once Pepper and his brothers found out one is onto their lands—which they consider the entire town to be—so he probably knew what he was talking about.

Forewarned, but unheeding, we thus began what would become the hardest outdoor slog of our careers. We took Pete up to Northeast Carry and stayed in one of the cabins Gus used when he was trout fishing. We scouted Saturday afternoon and most of Sunday. There was a lot of moose sign around and when Gus tried his moose call at dusk, he got a couple of bulls to respond across the pond so we were pretty psyched. Pete? Well his face sure lit up when he heard the bulls answering. He just about had stars in his eyes. "This is wonderful," he said, "just wonderful. I've never been happier. Thank you so much for coming. I'm so excited."

The next morning we got off to a good start. We went back to where we'd heard the bulls the night before and we scouted back beyond the first tree line. It was very thick brush, but we came upon an old tote road and saw some fresh tracks, so fresh there was still water draining into them. We had a good plan, a good area, and good weather. You can't ask for more. We were into it big time with a lot of confidence and restrained excitement. What a thrill to be on the first legal Maine moose hunt in decades. Those slowly filling tracks made us feel like we knew what we were doing—always a good sign for a Maine Guide!

We had not gone one hundred yards down a tote road when out of the brush about sixty yards down the trail came a nice yearling bull, just the kind of animal Pete wanted. Gus and I seemed to see it at once and everything developed in slow motion. Pete raised his rifle.

Then suddenly and unrepentantly, a tremendous blast hit me in my ears and the concussion knocked me to the ground. I was stunned. What a digger I took, falling down onto the trail and my face went into the pine needles as I saw the moose running away fast. "Jesus Christ," I bellowed, "who the hell fired?" Pete apologized profusely. "Sorry, Snappy, sorry, I don't know what came over me, I'm plumb sorry."

I got to my feet and dusted myself off, my ears still ringing like crazy. Gus just stood there with a stunned look on his face. He was speechless. Pete hung his head, "Sorry, Snap, I'm super sorry. Do you think I hit him?"

"No" both Gus and I bellowed, no doubt driving away any other nearby moose. Then Gus added, "You missed him, and Snappy, by a mile. But let's collect ourselves and see where he goes, in this boggy mossy stuff, he shouldn't be hard to track."

The three of us took a few moments to let things settle and then started off after the yearling bull. At first it was very easy to track him. His hooves left solid imprints and in the boggy terrain, you could see the water draining into the tracks with each passing step. We trudged along, trying not to push him too hard, but at a steady pace, hoping he would slow down and stop.

We saw several times where he did stop and turn sideways, no doubt looking back at us. Then he would take off again. Not running fast or even looping, you understand, but not meandering either. The young bull had our measure. The bull kept up a slow, steady pace, always quartering away from us and farther into the swamp. His tracks got more and more filled with water and I knew we were losing him.

Still, we followed the moose for the better part of an hour when I finally said, "Look guys, we could follow him to Greenville but what are we going to do if we catch up to him, it's too far from the road? It's probably almost two miles from our truck. Let's go back."

Pete nodded. "It's some far, for sure." So we headed back making a big loop. On our wanderings, we had gotten into the habit of looking into the beaver bogs for moose and had seen one cow that way so on the way back, we took turns looking into the various beaver bogs.

One time, I crawled through some thick brush because I heard some splashing and when I looked into the beaver bog, the whole side of the shore was black. I couldn't believe it. The moose's head was under water but it was the biggest moose I'd ever seen in the Maine woods. Just huge. I waited until he pulled his head up, the antlers looking over forty inches wide and dripping with pond lilies. What a monster head on him. The bull gave no sign he'd heard us and went back to feeding. I carefully backed out and whispered to the other guys.

"Pete, I know you didn't want this kind of moose and we're a friggin' hundred miles from the road, but I think if you take look at this moose, for the rest of your life, you're going to wish you'd shot him. He's amazing." Pete was beside himself with excitement as we changed places and he crawled in to take a look at the bull. I thought he was going to have a heart attack as he came back out. "My God, he's huge. He's a monster. We have to shoot him. Please."

I looked at Gus and he just shrugged, already having calculated what a haul it would be so I said, "Gus, you're the subpermittee, let Pete take the shot but you put another one in him right away. We don't want him wounded and running through that bog." Gus nodded and the two of them crawled into position. I watched as Gus counted with his fingers, 3-2-1. Then bang, bang, two shots almost as one rang out.

The moose fell over dead on contact. On contact with the bottom of the beaver bog that is. We had just dropped a 1200-pound moose into a 4-foot-deep beaver bog. He settled down, a gigantic black island in the middle of an inland sea. What a sight.

And what a mess. My God, I thought, we now have twelve hundred pounds of dead moose in four feet of water. It's about 65 degrees out, it's 11 a.m. and we're at least two miles from the road. We had just created an enormous task for ourselves. We stood there looking at the moose under water, but as I started to get ready to butcher it, Pete said, "I'm dying of thirst. Let's take a drink before we start carving him up."

"Don't," said Gus, with more than a little emphasis. "This water is like poison even before we start cutting up that moose and getting his guts out. Up by the Forks when I was trout fishing two summers ago, I drank some of that goddamned beaver water and wasn't I jeesly sick for three weeks. It's plumb awful stuff. It's nothing to fool around with, it even killed that Doc somebody who was head of the NRA. Don't mess with it."

Perhaps Pete wondered why two Maine Guides didn't have so much as a canteen between them but by then we were trying to clean out the moose. It was very important to avoid puncturing the paunch with several gallons of fermenting vegetable matter inside it. I don't believe any heart surgeon ever was more careful as we reached under several feet of water to cut loose the intestines and slowly, even delicately, floated them away like a huge smelly dirigible. We were extremely careful not to puncture the intestine walls either and pollute the meat. Or cause ourselves to pass out from the stench.

After we cut out the guts and floated them away downstream, we then had to skin the huge beast in place in order to cool the meat. Finally it fell to us to junk up the moose into manageable pieces and carry it all out to the truck.

My God that was hard work.

We even made it harder on ourselves by cutting down a long pole and trying to carry the hide out on it, thinking we were Indians on a portage. What a bad idea that was. Every step we took, the hundred pounds of wet moose hide swung back and forth, torqueing right and left, causing us great distress.

Through it all Pete was really a brick. Wounded as he had been in both legs and his back in Vietnam, he walked with some difficulty and this effort must have been sheer torture. But he never complained that long, long afternoon and evening. Once we got the hide off and the meat cooling down a bit, we carved up the carcass and took it out to the road, making several long, arduous trips before a couple of other hunters joined in and agree to help in exchange for some of the meat.

Still it was an enormously hard slog. Carrying the meat in the high temperature and humidity was bad enough, but the ground was so uneven with a number of beaver bogs to traverse and a constant up and down motion strained all of our muscles.

Up and down we went, over logs and through brush, using the trails when we could but we were well over a mile from Gus's Land Rover as the crow flies. But we weren't crows. And we certainly weren't flying. Plus we had to wrap the insides of Gus's Rover up like a mummy before he would let us put any of the meat inside.

When we finally got back to Little Harmony the next day, Pepper heard about it; he was not impressed with our feat. In fact, he almost died laughing. "I always knew you two guys were dubs, I mean honest to God, what were you thinking of shooting a big moose that far back in the country? You guys is numb as two flounders. Why didn't you ride the roads like any sensible moose hunter and drop one next to the road? I've never heard of such a thing."

He did admit that the horns of Pete's moose looked "tolerable" but predicted eating that tough old moose would be just as difficult as getting it out of the woods. "You'll be begging for mercy before you run through that pile."

Once again, Pepper turned out to be right.

After a god-awful afternoon and evening, we did get Gus' Rover loaded up and took the moose to the tagging station in Greenville. It was one of the larger moose taken that first day with the horns measuring well over forty inches. We never did get to weigh all the meat with the hide and horns, but there was a ton of it for sure. Peter took enough for his freezer and gave the rest to Gus and me. That amount alone filled both of our freezers and an extra food locker up in Waldoborough.

The upshot was in our house alone we ate moose meat for almost a year and a half. The old bull was just as tough as we had all imagined it would, or could be. You couldn't just throw it on the grill and eat the steaks, you had to put it in something and marinate it for days or grind it up and add a lot of fat to make it edible. We had it so often as moose burgers and moose-getty what our kids would take one look at the meal and shake their heads. "These aren't real hamburgers, Mom, are they?"

One weekend both of them came to us and handed Sunny a fistful of their dollars. "Please, Mom, please buy some Chinese takeout. We can't eat any more moose. We just can't."

For years afterward when any of the kids at school would offer them moose sandwiches from their parents, they'd shake their heads and nod sagely. "No thanks. Been there. Done that. No fun. We'll stick to mac and cheese." Or they asked, "Moose? I hope it was a calf. My father is such a dub, he brought home one of the big tough ones."

Anyway, they weren't the only ones who found the moose tough going. Even the people we gave some to rebelled. Zapper, who was infamous on the *Lady Ann* for eating octopus the winter he fished off the Grand Banks. He was the only member of the crew to like it, or actually to eat it for that matter. Zapper always said that the key to cooking octopus was to "pound the piss out of it beforehand. Smash it over and over with a wooden mallet, then it's some good." Zapper said our moose meat "was as tough as a twenty-year-old octopus," which I guess was not a compliment.

For his part, Little Robert tried to feed the last of it to his dogs but that too was tough going. "I had to chew it first for Sandy Andy," he said. "Her teeth ain't what they used to be. Come to think of it, mine aren't either. I thank you kindly, Snap, you and Gus both, but I'll pass on any more of that moose meat of yours. The missus jugged it for two weeks and it still was tough. She only jugges coon and possum for a week and then you can cut them with a fork."

My neighbor Norm, the one who'd given me the six-month-old intelligence which led to my blizzard buck, was never one to mince words and he said, "I appreciate you thinking of me, Snappy, but you know that old recipe for sea duck—put it on a wooden plank, bake it for three hours on that plank and then throw away the duck and eat the board? Well, your moose is tougher than that plank or that duck, dontcha know?"

Anyway, that night, by the time we got moose checked in and all the meat and horns back to Gus's cabin, it was almost midnight and every muscle in all three of our bodies was crying out for pain relief. We had a lot of Jim Beam, but woke up being more sore then we ever remembered from before. What a slog it had been.

Of course Pete was thrilled, positively ecstatic, and he couldn't sleep all night. "A dream come true," he said over and over. Gus allowed as how the dream that had come true was probably Pete not just surviving the A Shau but this little adventure as well. "I don't know how he did it with two bum legs. He's a guy I'm proud to say I've hunted with. Nary a complaining word. He's an inspiration, Snap, a tried and true inspiration."

One interesting sidelight, a few years later some wag at the Maine Fish and Game department thought that cutting your moose up out in the deep woods and bringing the little pieces to the game tagging station might well lead to abuses with different hunters bringing out pieces of several moose instead of just the one permitted.

I've never been clear how that would have been a big problem, but anyway, this guy got a rule passed that if you brought the moose out in pieces, you had to bring out four hooves if it was a bull and—I'm not making this up—if it was a cow, you had to bring out the uterus.

Now, I have honestly known a lot of hunters, maybe even a shit load of hunters, who would have a hard time identifying a human uterus in broad daylight, but getting the uterus of a moose right? No way. You should have seen the portions of the cow moose some nimrods tried to turn in to the tagging station. We talked to some guys from Fish and Game later and they said the nimrods had brought out all manner of cow moose parts. Wardens had seen kidneys, parts of intestines, lungs, and a variety of parts of the moose even they couldn't identify, but only occasionally, and then most probably by accident, an actual uterus.

The good news, they said, was no hunter had yet brought out a penis, claiming it was a uterus. Gus says this shows clearly that while they may have only a dim idea of the female anatomy, most hunters clearly have some familiarity with their own parts.

And this has translated well for their understanding of male moose parts as well.

chapter
eight

Blue Fish Blitz

"**I DON'T BELIEVE** a word of it," Pepper kept saying as he gestured wildly at the ceiling of Becky's Diner. He and Little Robert were having breakfast with Robbie when I came through the door. I soon found out that Pepper was going on about the "misinformation" that was being put out by Librarian Phoebe Pendergast. "The Widow keeps coming back with all sorts of nonsense from that woman; I wished she'd never gotten on that gd library job. Now Phoebe is saying the early settlers had so many lobsters that poor people wouldn't even eat them, prisoners either. I don't believe a word of it. I've never met anyone who would take corn meal mush over lobster, whether they were poor or not.

"It's like that time she told everybody the Indians went out sword fishing in their canoes. I mean to tell you, I've gone long lining once or twice for swords myself and I can tell you no christly canoe, birch bark or otherwise, is going to keep you above water when you're spearing a sword. Or trying to spear a sword and off Monhegan to boot? Never happened. That much I do know," Pepper said.

"Even the time she had that display on Malaga, she only got it half right for crumbs sake. I told her the story wasn't just about the state's lousy treatment of the black folks; it's that she skipped the whole part about how the sailors from Little Harmony would go there for their R and R on the way home. My grandpappy claimed, 'We always swung in there on the way home from the Grand Banks for a night or two. Our town was dry and Malaga was not. Most assuredly it was not. Sailing close hauled with a full load of fish, we'd hit that place some hard. Malaga teemed with lawlessness and loose women in those days don't cha know, thank the Lord. It was a damn shame when the state shut that colony down. It was fiercely enjoyable to pull in there after five or six weeks at sea, I'll tell you that. Not a damn preacher in sight, at least not one we ever recognized.'

"Now why the hell that woman couldn't put that part in, I'll never know. It's a town library after all."

In our town of Little Harmony, of course, there is a saying, "You can always tell a lobsterman, but you can't tell him much." Pepper is living proof that adage has more than a touch of truth. Unless those guys see it with their own eyes or hear it on the two-way from some highliner, they do not believe it. Even then it's 50-50 they'll choose to not believe it, except maybe if they hear it from another lobsterman on the CB. Even then, maybe not. Librarian Phoebe had been fighting a losing battle on her educational efforts for some time now.

Pepper grinned. "Well, Snappy, you've been mistook for an Indian, what do you think? Do you seriously think those Injuns did all that?" I laughed grimly for I knew where this conversation was going. Ever since I'd used a dead road kill possum for lobster bait (and it drew six lobsters, including two keepers), I'd been suspect in the eyes of a fair number of local watermen. For years afterward, they'd kid me about it.

"I think he's nuts, imagine if folks found out we was catching them bugs with road kill, I mean they'd never eat lobster again," avowed Zapper most loyally at the time. "But he's still my friend."

Pepper was a tad more direct about that incident. "Snappy, you are numb as a flounder if you think people will want to buy lobsters that have been caught on road kill, or bricks soaked in kerosene for that matter. You stop it right now."

Now Pepper was just getting warmed up on the sighting of me as an Indian. He got started with enthusiasm. "It's a damn good thing there was no female critter around to witness that spectacle of you in the all-together, but I'll tell you this, if there had been, Phoebe would have had you up on charges, or at the very least revoked your library card for sure."

But the Indian medicine man story, that was over the top as far as Pepper and all the Johnsons were concerned. I thought the story would fade away by and by but in a small town, the half-life of a story about a crazy person is about two generations, maybe three.

It had all started harmlessly enough. I had just gotten home from guiding with Gus up around Jackman. We'd taken three sports trout fishing and it had not gone well. The water was high and the mosquitoes and black flies were horrendous and the sports couldn't catch fish to save their souls.

Now I will always defer to Gus on fly fishing, but I'd be happiest if all I ever had to do to catch trout was to use worms. On this trip he did have a hellish time matching insect hatch with trout. I'll say that.

After the long ride from the Forks after the sports finally left, I'd taken a long hot shower and was about to sit down to dinner when my wife Sunny said, "Snap, there are a ton of bluefish going by our dock."

Well I leaped out of the shower with only a towel wrapped around me and grabbed my spinning rod. "I'll just catch one, hon," I said. She lost no time in answering, "Snap, dinner is almost on the table, do not take long or I'll hide you.

Remember Digger is coming tomorrow to go blue fishing; you promised to take him so don't wear yourself out tonight."

"Course not, Sunny, I won't even get dressed. I'll just catch one." I ran down to the dock barefooted and with only the towel around my waist, jumped into the wooden skiff. There was about three inches of water in the bottom of the boat after the rain while I was away, but I didn't even bother to bail it out.

I was in a real sweat to get that nice big blue fish instead of the small finicky trout I'd been friggin' around with the last three days. I just pulled the motor cord once and took off after the school of bluefish which was commencing to destroy a mess of pogies right there in front of me. Only two casts later with my Rebel and I had a bluefish on and I was reeling him in. Got him into the boat and was about to head for home.

But I just couldn't leave. I tried but I just couldn't bring myself to pull off the action. There were no other boats around. The blues were working themselves up into a true frenzy. Swirling, coming up under the pogies, slashing into them, fighting over the dead carcasses.

There was no way was I going to pull off that flurry with only one blue. For sure. I drifted with the current and the school up the bay. The towel was none too securely fastened so I had to keep having to stop and pull it up to retie it every other cast, but I hooked two more blues and managed to boat one of them. He slashed and bit like crazy and he caught me good in the finger as I was trying to unhook him and my finger began to bleed real good. But I finally ripped him off the tremble hook and threw him in the bottom of the boat. Then I hit him with an oar. That quieted him down a bit.

Then I hooked another one. This one took a long time to get into the boat and he just sort of fell off as he came over the gunwale. He was splashing around in bilge water flapping like crazy so I got the good idea to stand up on the seat so he couldn't bite me, him being some angry at being in a boat instead of outside it.

After all I was still barefooted. I swayed back and forth on the seat, trying to adjust the towel and cast ahead into the school. The bluefish were still slashing and mashing away, destroying pogie after pogie, some of which were floating dead on the water as the blues went after their cousins.

I kept drifting and casting, getting farther and farther away from my house. I did think guiltily about Sunny and her waiting dinner—but only briefly I admit. Dinner could wait. I had all winter to be on time for dinner. By now I was in as much of a feeding frenzy as the blue fish. I recognize that now as harmful but not at the time, no sir I did not.

Then on the next cast, my rod broke. It just snapped as two blues hit the same big blue and white Rebel popper and struggled to pull it every which way. I got down on my hands and knees and slowly pulled in the line, grabbing the wire leader at last and horsing the two blues into the boat. This time I didn't bother to try to unhook them; I took the broken rod as a sign from the gods of the outdoors it was time to go home.

However, then I discovered that standing on the middle seat, I could only barely reach the cord on the motor and I when I gave it a good, if awkward, yank the motor didn't turn over. Then I gave it another. Then another. Nothing. The motor would not turn over as I couldn't get enough purchase on the cord. So I sat down and took stock of the situation. I said to myself, "This hunt has blown up, I should row for home."

Still, the waters all around the boat were continuing to churn with blues and of course there were now six or seven blues *in* the boat, some of whom were still swimming around gnashing their teeth. "What the hell," I said to myself, "I can still jig for them by hand."

So I cut off the lure with the two blues on it and rigged another wire leader and put it on the line with a new lure. As soon as I threw that over the side, I hooked another blue and by the time I got that one in the boat, it was dark and the mosquitoes were out some fierce.

As the moon rose, my arms were aching and I was being bitten all over still having on nothing but that towel by now a really wet and limp towel. It was then I got the bright idea of splashing the bloody oily water from the bilge all over me.

That bloody, oily water did seem to give the skeeters pause but now I was covered with a greasy, fishy smelly film and the towel was soaking wet. I was bug bit, cold, and my arms and shoulders ached like crazy.

I was having the time of my life.

No way was I stopping yet.

That's how it came to pass that as I drifted around the end of the island and into the channel, hopping around on the middle seat, covered with slime and waving my arms to ward off skeeters and trying to keep casting my lure with no rod assistance at all.

So there I was in full moonlight when Captain Otis Macomb, a spry eighty-eight years young and inveterate waterman, came chugging along in his lobster boat, the *Joyce M.* He thus saw a scene which did seem a tad out of the ordinary, even with his long years of experience of being on the water.

"I thought it was a jeesly Indian, a medicine man," he told one and all at the town landing when he arrived that night. "Or the ghost of one. He was a jumping around, waving his arms and chanting some Indian gibberish. I never seen the like. When I found out it was Snappy, well sir, I thought he'd lost all his marbles."

Even Otis's young stern man, Mitch who'd had a few cold ones after they unloaded their catch allowed as how, "It looked damn strange, a damn sight stranger than anything I'm used to. We'd had a long day, for sure, I mean that's no excuse but it was damned odd. For shit sure it was plumb odd. It spooked me. I thought all the Injuns around here were dead or gone up country. I thought Livey who died was the last of them in this town so it was some kind of spooky sight, I'll tell you that. When I heard him cavorting around like that I thought he was casting a spell on us. And with our luck lately with catching the bugs, we did not need anything more to plague us."

Of course neither of them stopped to see if I needed help, just gawked and drank their beer and then moved on. Soon I was alone in the moonlight again with the bugs and the bilge full of bluefish and a ton of bluefish still chomping away all around the boat. So back I went to fishing and I caught two more before I then lost that lure when the line snapped and the bluefish carried the whole rig down the channel.

About that time another boat came alongside. It was my neighbor Tommy. "I'm not one for giving you advice this time of night, Snap," he said, "but if I was you I'd let me tow you back to your dock. Sunny is more than peeved and you know that woman is not one for blowing smoke. In fact, I've never seen her so pissed. I'd say you're going to be sleeping in the barn tonight. That is after you clean all these blues. My God what a mess. You're covered with blood and slime and shit, what have you been doing?"

Tommy laughed all the way back to my dock, shaking his head as I stood glumly on the seat atop about ten bluefish in various stages of mortification, but with me still not sure they were all dead and so unwilling to put my bare feet back down on the floorboards. I rode home standing on the seat, admiring the moon and wondering what I was in for.

And Tommy was right about Sunny of course. She is a wonderful woman and slow to anger, but this was some true provocation.

Even I had to admit that.

There on the door was a nice, short and measured note. "Supper in the barn. Stay there. PS Remember Digger will be here at first light." Well, luckily I had a half bottle of Jim Beam out in the barn or it would have been an even more uncomfortable night. By the time I got all the fish cleaned and in the freezer and had my cold supper and done a number on the Jim Beam, I got into my truck and lay down to take what turned out to be a very short nap.

Before I knew it, and with a truly monumental hangover headache, I heard Digger arrive. "Christ, Digger, it's hardly dawn," I managed to get out. "Let's get going, Snappy, time's a wasting."

The sun was just peeping over the horizon, but even that much light was too much for my tortured eyeballs and I commenced to close them as much as I could. Luckily Sunny didn't hold my night escapade against Digger and insisted he have breakfast. I gobbled down the flapjacks with a ton of life-fulfilling maple syrup and avoided her flashing eyes.

As I took a handful of Advil and drank a ton of orange juice, I wondered how I was going to get through that day. What agony. All self-inflicted I realized. Knowing that didn't help any for sure. I just wanted to stay home and finish my bath from the night before and get some sleep.

The problem was I owed Digger a lot. He was one of the top guides in the state, a lifelong dedicated hunter and fisherman and he'd taken my boy Jack under his wing when he got interested in the out of doors. He took Jack fresh water fishing and in one whirlwind of a day, they caught smelts, sunfish, yellow perch, eels, pickerel, and even a lake trout. "That boy doesn't care what he catches, just as long as he horses them into the boat. You won't go hungry with that lad afield," he'd said, grinning.

And when it came time for Jack to hunt, once he passed his safety course, Digger took him out and showed him a pair of moose and even put him on a big 8-pointer down in a cedar swamp. Jack was so surprised when the deer exploded in front of him, he never fired a shot but he was very impressed that Digger knew where to take him for such a chance. And so was I. I never went hunting with Digger but what he got us within sight of some whitetails even if they were does or yearlings. He was uncanny good with deer, that's for sure.

Digger had gotten his name early in life. He was in the seventh grade and his dad Ezra took him out after school. In those days, he brought his shotgun to school and kept it in his locker right in the hallway so he could hunt on the way home.

Ezra was, and still is, one of the grand old men of the Maine out of doors. Last Christmas we got a card from him at age ninety. There he was, as big as life, sitting on the front of the Christmas card in hunter orange from head to toe, turkey hunting under a tree. The inscription said, "Heaven Can Wait. Merry Christmas. Ezra." What a hoot. What a grand gentleman he was. I've always been grateful that I had a chance to know Ezra and hunt with him, thank the Good Lord.

Anyway on the way home from school with his shotgun and deer slugs, Digger found some tracks and followed them up the mountain. Surprised a big buck just as the light was going and hit him hard behind the shoulder, but like so many whitetails do when hit, the buck ran down the hill trying to get into the black growth. Some excited, Digger ran after him and tripped on a tree root. What a wicked digger he took splitting open his chin and his forehead both. It took 14 or so stitches to close the wounds, but not before Digger, blood streaming down his face, caught up with the wounded buck and finished him off. The doctor in the ER said, "That's quite a digger you took young man." The name stuck and as Ezra said, "Stuck with pride."

So as we're having breakfast and Digger was really excited. He doesn't get to do much in salt water and I'd told him about the blues being in and thick this summer. So thick in fact that the blues were slaughtering pogie school after pogie school all over Little Harmony. The stench and vapors from the dead pogies was so bad in some coves that the paint peeled off the seaward houses. It was a hell of a mess. That summer I'd seen pogies swimming out of the water going across the marsh grass trying to get away from those masses of blue fish bent on mass destruction. A fish out of water swimming on land, terrorized out of its mind, is not something you see every day although perhaps you'd like to. I know I would.

But it sure made for super fishing that glorious summer.

So after breakfast we got the boat cleaned up and then I got my one bright idea of that last 24 hours. I admit to being like a trout myself. Primitive. Single minded. Not prone to grand schemes. Focused on simple things. Besides my head hurt like hell and I wasn't able to muster any grand thoughts even if it had been my way. I did say to myself, "I hope those blues have them pogies penned up in one of the coves near where they were last night. I'll bet they're back in one of those coves herding those suckers and getting ready to feed on them again. They must have stopped eating sometime and where were those pogies going to go, the blues were all around them?"

So once we got the boat squared away and started the motor—on the first pull don't you know—when I stood in front of it properly, my feet on the deck, not the seat. We headed up the bay and behind the island to where I'd broken off from the blues. I hoped they hadn't held that against me. But Mother Nature sometimes does hold it against you when you're into the fish or the game and you break off for any reason.

But not this time. As soon as we rounded the bend I saw that there was movement under the water by the point. Not the thrashing, splashing, volcanic eruptions of last night, but some minor turbulence and an occasional black fin of the bluefish patrolling the entrance to the cove. They'd gone and gotten the pogies penned up in that cove.

I pointed to the opening of the cove and said, "I'd cast over there Digger to see if they're at home." Digger got all excited and wound up a hell of a cast. He'd come loaded for bluefish—or deep sea fishing in any case. He had a sturdy trolling rig with a nice red and white Rebel. The Rebel flew about ten feet and plopped dead in the water.

I didn't say anything, just put on a humongous big popper, I figured the bluefish had fed all night and weren't really going to be all that hungry so I'd have to rile them up some.

I threw the popper way ahead of the boat, almost to the rocky point and it fell with a huge splash. Instantly a bluefish charged at it and missed, but a second one nailed it. "Fish on," I called out, somewhat unnecessarily.

As I played the fish, I kept looking out of the corner of my eye at Digger. He was fuming and kept trying to cast but with his rig, he just couldn't reach the school no how, no way. I knew he was not about to ask to use my rod but he was in true agony, big bluefish within a few yards of him and he powerless to get to them.

I boated that first fish and handed him my spinning rod. "Here, Digger, take mine. I'm plumb worn out from last night." You would have thought I'd just given him a million dollars. "Thanks, Snap," he said, "this is quite a sweet rig." Of course if it had been a tree limb but it got the popper over to the blues, he would have praised that rig as well.

And so it was. He cast the popper and trailed it back toward the boat. It hadn't come back ten feet from where it landed when a big bluefish tore into it and Digger had his first action of the day. It was a delight for the next hour or so, he landed a half dozen blues.

For my part, I drank two of his cold Buds and I felt much, much better. The smile on Digger's face didn't hurt either. A few weeks later Digger wrote a long article on the adventure for the *Maine Sportsman* and I felt real good about the whole deal. Of course, I let Digger have all the bluefish, I'd had enough of cleaning them the night before to last me a long while.

And Sunny? Well I took her out to her fancy Italian restaurant in Portland and she never mentioned the incident during dinner except to say "Digger sure had a good time. I'm glad you let him have all the fun and didn't try to hog it all like you sometimes do." That girl sure has a wry sense of humor. I've said that more than once.

But over dessert, she accepted my apology when I declared earnestly, "I'm sorry I provoked you." Then she reminded me about the time that Gus and I brought home two hundred pounds of bear meat unexpectedly one warm night after the sport we'd taken up near Daaquam Station got his spring bear but then didn't want the meat. We dropped him off at the airport and arrived in Sunny's kitchen about 8 p.m. with the meat. We had to do something with the meat right away so she, Gus and I proceeded to bring it into our "fish room" and stood there cutting up the meat and drinking gin and tonics until well after midnight. For the next year, any and all guests were served bear meat. A little is very tasty, but goes a long way.

"Now that, Snappy, in my book was a real provocation," Sunny said.

As for the blues, they stayed around for another couple of weeks, destroying schools of pogies and causing piles of dead fish to build up on various shorelines. People who didn't fish raised hell and even asked the governor to do something about the mess.

But of course, as Zapper and Little Robert are fond of saying, things always turn out poorly when government gets involved. "Ain't it odd, things just naturally fall apart when those idjets get their snouts involved." Governor McKernan, who was a fine fellow in many ways, foolishly listened to the laments of those who had paint peeled off their houses and not the guys who wanted the blues to come back and do damage like that every year. McKernan, well he upped and signed some sort of agreement with the Russkies and they brought over some factory ship the next summer and got to buy all the pogies in sight. Tons of them. And more tons. Local guys made a shit load of money and the Russkies? Well they filled that big sucker of a mother ship three times over. After that there was no more paint peeling along the shore.

And no more pogies.

And, of course, damned few blue fish after that either.

I mean, if you're a blue fish, you don't come to Maine for the summer art festivals. And you don't come for the antiques. You come for those luscious pogies and when there aren't any pogies worth swimming north of the Cape Cod Canal for, well then you don't swim much north of the Cape Cod Canal. It seems that simple.

I swear it *is* that simple. We Mainers can blame the Masshole commercial fishermen for taking all those striped bass year after year what with a law against taking striped bass but no fine if you do.

But we have nobody to blame for the blue fish drought but those damn bureaucrats who thought some minor smell and peeling paint on a few houses was worth the true joy of Maine fishermen catching a shit load of those magnificent fighting machines, the murdering, massacring, heartless, jeesly lovable blue fish.

I'd rather eat a striped bass any day for sure, but I'd much, much rather catch a blue fish. And I'm not alone in that I reckon. Just ask any true bay man or woman. Blue fish are true savages at heart. And so are we.

Even Pepper agreed that he would have stayed to slay those blues that night. "But Sunny had every right to shut you off though when you didn't. Fair is fair."

Well said, Pepper.

Life Lessons of Old Rope and Livey Huntley

MY GRANDSON Dusty and I were sitting on our porch that fine spring morning enjoying a much frowned upon Classic Coke when Gus roared up, jumped out of his Rover, and said, "Snap, damn it, I will not do it."

"Damn is a bad word, Uncle Gus," Dusty said. His kindergarten teacher, Ms. Francine Malware, is death on bad words. So far she has stricken "dumb," "retarded," "clumsy," and "fat," "stupid," and "nuts" from poor five-year-old Dusty's vocabulary. "By the time he's in high school he will be some tongue tied. Or at least unable to communicate with 75 percent of the kids in our town—let alone those dung-eyed farmers up country Bowdoinham way. For sure," exclaimed Gus.

Ms. Malware did run into a buzz saw with Dusty's mom, Dee Dee, when she told the kids it was wrong to hunt. Dee Dee, who passed her hunter safety course when she was in the seventh grade and won a prize the following year for a report on "The Right to Arm Bears?" Dee Dee commenced to roar down there the next day before school and tore into Ms. Malware some good.

"If there is one thing we Mainers cannot stand," she said fiercely, "it is oafish people from away like you downing our traditions. You shape up and fly right starting right now or the school board will be getting a visit from me and Willimina Sessions. You will not be pleased if Willa gets involved, I can promise you that much."

That put an end to the anti-hunting chatter in the lower grades, at least for a while but that battle never seems to end.

But back to the springtime story.

"I'm sorry, Dusty," Gus said, "but I do not care. I do not care what law the Legislature of the Great State of Maine passes, I will not put my mouth on my sport's mouth. I will stop guiding. I honestly will for God's sake."

"What do you mean?" I asked, flabbergasted.

"They did it. They just passed a gd law that says we guides have to give mouth to mouth resuscitation to any sport who has a heart attack or stroke out in the woods. Good Christ. I will not do it."

Well, I had to admit it gave me some pause too, what with some of the yahoos we took afield. The very thought of giving them the breath of life was, well, nerve wracking. And, weird as it sounds, I could just hear Pepper when he found out, "You and Gus deep kissing some christly sport who keeled over in the woods. Shit, I will pay real money and pass up on kissing Lady Helga to watch that shit. I promise you." I knew he would too.

On the other hand, there was one Maine Guide, the legendary Lash Harvey from Washington County, who might relish the new law. Early in his career, he focused on female sports and now almost exclusively catered to that clientele. Even women couples got star wattage treatment from Guide Lash Harvey. I could just hear one of his female sports saying, "But, Lash, I think I only sprained my wrist, I do not need any mouth to mouth resuscitation."

"I do declare you have a point, Gus. I'd hate to give up guiding but this could do it. This might be some serious. How the hell did it happen?" asked Dusty.

"Well Spike McCoy up Mt. Vernon way, lost a sport up on the mountain last winter. Wouldn't give him mouth to mouth after the jeesly old guy had a heart attack. I guess he had really foul breath and all so the next session, the sport's family made a huge stink about it and gol-durn it, don't you think those piss-ants passed a law."

Dusty looked like he was about to correct Uncle Gus on "piss-ants" but instead he seemed to want to keep the conversation going. "But why did you guys become a Maine Guide in the first place?" Dusty asked.

I thought for a while, hoping Gus might chime in but he was too agitated and just excused himself and headed off to hit hard that special single malt he kept on hand for such-like disasters. I could see he really was shook up over this business of giving sports mouth to mouth. It could be the end of an era, for sure if Gus decided to pack it in.

Dusty sat waiting patiently for an answer.

"I've never really thought about it too much before, but you know, Dusty, I can think of a few reasons. One would be a man named Old Rope. Another would be an Indian who taught me a lot about the out of doors, Livey Huntley. And then, truth be told, I guess I'd have to throw in old L.L. Bean himself although I wouldn't want that part to get out."

Dusty looked interested in hearing the story, or at least fascinated by the Classic Coke can I opened and handed to him as I popped the tab on my own. At home he was never, ever, allowed to scoff down any beverage with sugar in it, let alone one laced with caffeine and who knows what else that makes it so frigging addictive.

I am morally certain that little cuss listened to everything I had to say in the hope that I would keep mainlining that "very bad for you but delicious and soul lifting beverage." But he kept slurping on his can and following the conversation.

"Well," I said, after sucking down half of my own ice cold Classic Coke in three quick gulps. "I realized what he meant to me when I saw a sign in our town dump one day. It said, 'Am Sick. Go Home. Old Rope.'"

I flashed back to those six words scrawled on a piece of plywood at the town dump. Our old smoldering open town dump. Smelly. Unhygienic. Trash filled, garbage overflowing, rat-infested town dump. Actually it was a glorious place to learn how to shoot. All that other stuff was merely the background, the ticket of admission to a fantastic world.

It was Old Rope's words that really mattered, then and now. How odd those words sound today reverberating across the decades. They had a huge impact on my life. Am Sick. Go Home. Old Rope.

And to this very day, I am embarrassed, even ashamed that I do not know Old Rope's real name. I only know he died as he lived, on the fringes of society and poor by any standards, even those of fifty years ago.

He was a "marginal" man in terms of society and yet, he had a profound impact on me and others and certainly on my becoming a Maine Guide. Life is truly odd, often when you least expect it. I hadn't thought about Old Rope for years. But Dusty's question stirred me up. A lot.

I thought for a moment and said, "Well, it really started with Old Rope." "Who was Old Rope?" Dusty asked. "He turned out to be a very important person in my life, although at the time I had no idea he was or ever would be."

"How could that be, Snappy?" Dusty continued. "Well," I said, "nobody in my family hunted and although my father took my cousin and me fishing a lot, he wasn't into hunting even though we had a ton of guns around the house.

"But Old Rope, Dusty, he was something else. I don't know if he knew Livey, but they sure spoke the same language to me. They both were tuned into nature in the way most people are not and I think that really, really influenced me.

"When I was in high school, some of the guys would go to the town dump after school to shoot rats and that's how I met Old Rope. A lot of kids in those days had BB guns and some of us were lucky enough to graduate to having .22s. That was a real rite of passage in those days, to leave the BB guns behind and get a real gun. They were mostly single shot rifles, although I soon got hold of a big old Mossberg .22 which held eight or ten rounds with one loading. Actually it was a pretty dangerous firearm, you never knew how many shells were in it. But it was a sweet little autoloader for that time. My uncle almost accidentally shot my grandmother with it, but that's another story," I said.

"Now, Dusty, in those days, which were long before recy-cling centers and all that sorting of trash, people brought their trash to the dump and threw it on a big smoldering pile of waste. Even if you had somebody else pick up your garbage and bring it to the dump, it still got tossed on this constantly smoking and burning pile of waste.

"That pile was always smoldering and on fire and gave off a fearsome odor, but then, we didn't think it was bad, we just thought that's the way things were. Now of course with all that edible trash and open acres and acres of junk, there were a lot of rats.

"Old Rope encouraged us kids to bring our .22s and shoot the rats as they scrambled around on the old, burned tin cans. The first time I went to the dump, I was hooked. Standing there with a rifle and having a bunch of rats roiling around and having you and your buddies getting ready to shoot at them, it was so much fun. It was a real life video game like you kids play today. Except it was for real. I went day after day and that's really how I learned to shoot."

Now Old Rope was down on his luck and very poor even though he picked a lot of trash from the dump. He might not have been a role model by today's standards, but in the 1950s he was somebody to listen to. He'd take his time showing us how to shoot those rats, how to lead them, their habits and he always got a kick out of our excited cries, "I got one."

"Maybe because I went there a lot and maybe because I always was respectful of him and asked him questions about how he picked the dump. 'Copper beats iron, you remember that.' When I looked puzzled, he added, 'You can have a passel of iron and I'll take a little copper and I'll come out ahead every time,' he'd say and then take the time to explain why. He always was patient with me explaining the out of doors facts of life. I wasn't much of a shot to start but I kept at it and he'd help me understand things like leading the rats when they were running."

I went on to tell Dusty how once, Old Rope took me and another kid, Arty Pritchard, aside and said, "You guys come back tonight after dark. We'll have some fine shooting then." Arty and I hadn't figured out that the rats really came out at night but when we arrived that night, we heard them rummaging around, running over the burned cans and creating quite a commotion. "Wish we could shoot them," Arty said, and Old Rope grinned his toothless grin. "Well, boys, I'm about to show you. You brought your guns, right?"

We had brought our guns and Old Rope brought out a couple of old flashlights he'd salvaged, saying, "These were thrown away but I fixed them and put in new batteries." He then taped them to the barrel of our guns with white adhesive tape and we were in business.

"What a thrill, Dusty," I continued, "wherever the light shown was a target area and in the dark, there were dozens and dozens of targets as the rats ran hither and yon. It took some getting used to, the wavering light and swinging the rifle from side to side and hitting a rat as he, or she, sat up and looked at the light.

"But what a blast. We shot three boxes of .22 shells that first night and from then on, most of any money we earned went for shells. Old Rope delighted in our enthusiasm and our willingness to blast away over and over. From that moment on, I wanted to be a hunter. I loved the excitement of the hunt and the kill. Rats were bad and caused diseases, and we were doing a good thing to thin out their population, Old Rope told us that. We'd never kill enough of them to wipe them out either, he insisted." Turns out he was right.

"Dusty," I said, "rats were not then, nor are they now, nor have they ever been, an 'endangered species.' And if by chance they should ever become endangered, almost no one would ever say, 'That's too bad.' They would be much more likely to say "god speed,' that is if anybody dared to say that kind of thing today out loud.

"Over time, I got pretty good at it, Dusty, and when Old Rope told me what a fine shot I was, I was really proud. I'd bring my best friends like my cousin Dave from Portland and let him try. Dave thought it was so cool to shoot at a dump like that and allowed as how he wished Portland had such a fine place for a gun club to meet.

"What a disappointment then when I tried out for the high school rifle club and didn't make the team. I was heartbroken. That night at the dump, I told Old Rope and he patted me on the head and said, 'Kid, there are two kinds of shooters in the world. Some, they can hit paper targets. Other is ones who can hit something with fur or feathers. You be one who needs feathers and furs. You have the makings of a good Mountain Man, that is if we still had any real ones around today.'

"I felt much better about myself then and admitted that I really didn't like the dark, dank firing range under the YMCA and those little paper targets were pretty boring after shooting those rats and watching them spin over and over after you blasted them." I paused for a sip of Coke.

"Dusty, Old Rope was very important to me in those teenage years. He taught me how to trap in the ponds out behind the dump and he patted me on the back the first day I caught a water rat in a trap baited with a carrot. He did say they didn't taste as good as a muskrat or possum but that he'd eaten them on occasion. He also did not recommend me bringing it home to my parents, as proud as I was of my catch. He would say, 'Yesteryear a man could make a good living trapping. Not anymore. Them critters is mostly in decline.'"

I told Dusty how very sad I was one Friday afternoon one October day when I went to the dump and there was a painted sign by Old Rope's little shack. "It said 'Am Sick. Go Home. Old Rope.' The next day, we found out that Old Rope had been sick, and he had gone home and he had died of a heart attack. My friends and I were really sad for a long time. Old Rope was a true friend and we missed him a lot. We still went to the dump and shot rats but it wasn't the same."

I continued. "As for Livey, well knowing him, I got to hang out with one of the few left Indians in Little Harmony. Livey Huntley sure influenced me a lot. I wanted to be like him when I grew up, at least when I was seven or eight."

"Snappy, you said Livey was an Indian. Our teacher told us 'Indian' is a bad word too. You're supposed to call a person like them a Native American."

"Well, you're right, today you are, I guess you are, but in the fifty years I've been in the Maine woods, I've never ever heard anyone use the term 'Native American,' including Native Americans. I've heard a few like Rascal and Ivor use some other words, especially when they've got a snoot full, but I've never heard 'Native American' spoken of in the woods."

"Not even by a Native American?" he quizzed. "Nope, maybe today Indians would call themselves that, but not all those years ago. Livey Huntley called himself an Indian, and he was proud to call himself that he said. Maybe today he'd look at it different, but then Livey said he was an Indian and that was that. But I never heard anyone say a disrespectful word about Livey. We all envied his bush craft and knowledge. He was a hell of a guy. We'd have called him 'Sir' or anything else if that's what he wanted.

"You know, lots of hunters and fishermen and women think they're pretty good in the out of doors. And certainly we Maine Guides do. We think we're pretty special and often pretend we would make out alright if we lived back in Colonial times. Maybe we would, but you know, I doubt it. As much time as we spend in the woods and as much as we learn over a lifetime tramping around, I don't believe it's the same as really living off the land, truly, 365 days a year.

"And I know we don't know as much as the average teenage Abenaki brave, let alone his father or his grandfather. No sir, Dusty, we all are just playing at being an Indian, that's what I think. Now we like to play at it, and some of are better than others playing at it, but we are still just playing at it," I said.

"But being introduced to the out of doors by an Indian, well that was pretty special. I was about ten when Livey showed up at our house. My father was a carpenter and he had a band saw in the basement and Livey brought over a deer to have him cut it up on the band saw. It was out of season I guess, not that I knew or cared at the time. Livey was tall and strong and very gentle with us kids and patient too, showing us plants that could heal and mushrooms that would make you sick. He was the most patient adult I knew. Livey'd answer all our questions, serious like, and after we got to know him, he'd take us along the shore as well as into the woods and show us the tracks and the wild things you could eat and how to find your way. He would have made a great dad.

"Just having him as a friend made you a big deal in our little town. 'I saw you with Livey, what were you doing down by the pond?' kids would say. One year, Livey took me scalloping the opening day of the season and in those days, you could get off from school if you were going scalloping opening day, or at least that's what Livey told my parents. He came in his old truck before it was light and we were out on the water at dawn. My mother got up real early to make me bacon and eggs and feed Livey too.

"When we got to the bay, there were lots of other boats out, it being opening day and all, but Livey seemed to know just which patches of eelgrass held the most scallops. We got them in big wire nets and we were the first ones back at the dock with our three bushels. We weighed in and cashed out and Livey gave me $5 of the take. That was the most money I'd ever had in my life, and didn't I feel some proud when I went into school late, wearing my black boots and with a seagull feather in my cap and $5 in my pocket. I felt like a million dollars and the kids, even the ones who didn't like me, were impressed when I said, 'Yeh, we got three bushels by nine or so.'"

I told Dusty that after that I wanted to impress Livey more than just about anybody else I ever met in my whole life. I told Dusty that I always listened carefully to the lessons he was trying to teach me. One winter day, a deer swam across the bay through the floating ice opposite our house. I saw it a long way away and watched it swimming right to the rocks by in front of our house. I was so excited. I didn't have more than a BB gun then so I decided to capture it by roping it when it came ashore. I got my sister to help and when the deer finally staggered ashore and collapsed, she and I lassoed it and held on even though it tried to drag us along. We finally got her tied up when she fell over from exhaustion. Then I called Livey. I thought he would be so pleased.

"I guess he was, at least in a way, but when he arrived in his truck and I had a big kitchen knife all ready to kill the shivering doe, he said, 'No Jack, think of how far this deer swam and how much she wanted to live swimming all that way. She's probably going to have a fawn or two in the spring so I'd let her go free.

"'But it's your deer son,' he continued, 'and I'll do whatever you want and I do thank you for thinking of me. That sure took a lot of courage and no little skill to lasso that deer. Nope, I don't know any boys your age or many men for that matter who could have done it. So you have a lot to be proud of, but if it was me, I'd let her go. She deserves a chance to live and have her fawns.'

"Gulping hard and almost crying, I said, 'Sure, Livey. Sure, that's best. Maybe we could put her in your truck and drive her out in the woods.'

"'That's a great idea Jack, I'm going to do just that. I'm proud of you Jack, real proud.'

"So, Dusty, the three of us picked the doe up and put her in the back of the truck and he drove off with her. A few days later Livey came by and said, 'I drove up by Three Mile River and let her go. Your doe, she ran off going pretty good so I think she's going to be alright. You kids did alright. She might have broken her leg on those icy rocks. You kids kinda saved her I think.'

"I felt real good about myself then and of course how I looked in Livey's eyes. Livey would go on to teach me much much more about the out of doors, but what he'd taught me that day, that there was more to being a true son of nature than just catching and killing, has always struck in my mind."

In later years, of course I wondered if he already had enough deer meat in his freezer but when you're a kid, you're not that cynical. Either way, it was a great life lesson and when you're in the out of doors and hunting and fishing, ending up feeling good about yourself, whether you bring home the fish or the bird or the deer or not, that's what really matters, feeling good about being in the out of doors and doing Nature proud.

"But I think, Dusty, the key is, you cannot really be a good Maine Guide unless you love the critters you hunt. I know it sounds funny for they certainly, most certainly do not, love you back for trying to kill them and eat them, but all true guides, all true hunters for that matter, have to love what they chase or they would soon get tired of it. If you love the critters you will always want to know more about them and that will keep you going year in and year out. Or at least it did me."

"But, Snappy, neither of these guys was a Maine Guide, why did you want to become a Maine Guide?" Dusty asked. "Where did that come from?" The kid is relentless on questions, that's for sure. And maybe it was the second Coke he was working on.

"You know, it's kind of funny but that part came right from L.L. Bean. That's where I met my first Maine Guides. My father would take me and my cousin Charlie up there sometimes, especially around Christmas time. We'd sit around by the front desk and listen to the trappers and guides and hunters talking and boy, did we want to be like them. Them Maine Guides especially. Everybody treated them like they were something, even the trappers with the pelts still hanging off them."

"L.L. Bean? Are you sure, Snappy? You're always making fun of those Japanese tourists taking pictures of themselves by the L.L.Bean trout pond down there and calling it seeing the Wild, Wild East."

"Well in those days, L.L.Bean didn't have all the products and customers it has now. In those days it was just for out of doors guys and the gals that hung out with them. And hunting and fishing was the center of the store, not off in that other place the way they got it now. No, it was a different store then, that's for sure. Still, truth be told, old L.L. would have liked all the money the new store brings in. He always appreciated a buck, at least that's what the regulars always said.

"Honestly, Dusty, you'd sit there if you were a little kid and just listen. Some old codger would come through the door swinging a trap or two and they'd pull up a chair and light their pipe and stark yakking after they got their ammo or whatever they'd come in for."

"What do you mean light their pipe? Could they smoke in the store? Gosh, I never heard of that. How did they get away with that?"

I laughed. "Well times were different. So there would be hunters and fishermen and trappers and then there would be these guys who were Maine Guides. They often had red patches on their shoulders and the others sitting around would listen to them and ask them questions.

"Even L.L. Once I was there and he came in and they kidded and joked with him about the little caribou he'd shot and he'd fire right back, grinning, 'Well at least I shot a caribou, Hank. I've never seen any caribou antlers on your cabin wall. And it was shot legal too, which is more than I can say for some of the horns on the walls belonging to you all around layabouts.' But after he left, one of the guys said, 'L.L. is great fun to take out hunting. He takes direction some good. He's a regular guy. I like hunting with him. No airs about 'im.' 'Having no airs' is always a nice compliment from a Maine Guide," I said.

"Now maybe L.L. was never a Maine Guide himself but the respect he paid them made me want to be just like them. That's for sure. If the legendary L.L. thought they were special, well then I guess I thought they were too."

"So would you ever give it up like Gus? Give up being a Guide?"

"Well." I laughed. "I don't know, it beat the hell out of me, maybe that'll be a story for another day, but that law Gus says the Legislature just passed, well, I'm thinking of all those guys and gals I've taken out into the deep woods and I'm thinking, well, maybe it's just time to hunt or fish by myself or with Gus or with you kids. That kiss of life might taste real funny coming from some of the dubs I've hunted with if you know what I mean. Some of those guys, I just don't know how they would taste."

Dusty nodded as if in agreement. Then he added, "You don't think I could have another Coke, do you, Snappy?"

chapter
t e n

The Curse of the Beaver Lady

"**CRIPES BEAVERS** is numb, Snappy," Tadpole said. "Just plain numb. Think about it. They start cutting a tree and forget about it. They drop a big sucker of a tree, eat a few branches and wander off. They'll ring a tree and go about their business. They eat themselves out of house and home without any thought at all, leaving all that food for years on the ground to waste. Look at over Gus's place, look how many trees are half down and only partially chewed up. Beavers is numb. Plus those big orange teeth of them critters creep me out. They are some ugly. Born that way, no doubt."

The subject of beavers came up that Fourth of July on Saturday, the day of the parade. Pepper had sent Tadpole out to get some liquid refreshment and a half dozen Whoopie pies and he was having the devil's own time getting through the crowds. We bumped into each other by the fire station and he started in about the flappy tailed ones without much of any preamble. He was like his father, prone to jumping into a conversation full bore.

Now there are two schools of thought about beaver. In the abstract they are cute and industrious and they create some nice water reserves for all kinds of critters. Some even claim they make good eating although not Tadpole. "Tastes like newspaper," he said, "newspaper with a little fat in it." Still beavers can look fine and sleek, and even cute if you don't look too closely, and you can make a lot out of them and their cuteness.

Into this school of loving beavers fell Helga Merriman, wife of Captain Amos Merriman, the long liner out of our Spangler's Cove. Helga loved them, talked them up every chance she could, defended them against all comers. She even gave them pet names and always, always took their side. "They are just adorable and so loving and kind to each other. They are wonderful." Everybody in town, at least anybody who ever talked with Helga, heard that beavers were first rate critters, above average in intelligence, and really fine all around. She was their number one champion.

The other school, of course, agreed with Tadpole that they are just huge rodents, creatures who cause more harm than good. Yes, they dam up any running water, but in the process, they jam up culverts and flood roads and fields and they cannot be stopped, short of shooting them or trapping them. Above all, they are relentless cutting the hard wood until there is no more left around their lodges. They are numb enough to eat themselves out of house and home and they waste a shitload of timber. They also spread disease. Just ask Gus; twice he took to drinking water when he went trout fishing upcountry and, seduced by the look of the clear fresh water, he got that beaver shitting disease. Makes you think you have the flu and will never, ever get rid of it.

So at first glance, you might put Gus in the second camp. But you'd be wrong, there were three big ponds on Gus's property thanks to the beavers who built those big dams and raised the water level in them to five or six feet so he could put in trout and have a high old time, even bringing some city sports to catch a few trout at dusk on one of his beaver ponds.

Before he wandered off, I asked Tadpole where Norm Franklin was. Norm was Little Harmony's oldest war veteran and he'd always been on the first vehicle in the parade. I'd missed him today. Norm had been in World War I and had been feted ever since even though he spent most of his time during that war in supply depots around Paris. He did have some fine stories about the ladies of the night in lieu of combat tales, though, we all gave him that.

Tadpole, like his father, knew every snippet of gossip around Little Harmony so he laughed as he filled us in. "Well Phoebe Pendergast claimed she saw Norm exposing himself on the float during rehearsal yesterday and so they decided to put Norm inside the cab of the fire truck this year 'stead of up on one of the floats. Keep a sharp eye out, you might see his head but I doubt you will see the rest of him."

Now Phoebe was one of those people who in Salem at the time of the Pilgrims would have sat at the back of the church on Sundays with a long pole and whacked you if you fell asleep in church. She was also the Little Harmony town librarian AND the organizer of the Fourth of July parade. If she'd nailed Norm, he wasn't coming back, for her word was law. Everybody was afraid of her although when she ran for the state senate (no lower offices for her!) she didn't get many votes. "That woman would be running our lives from front to back and back to front," explained Little Robert. "It would be like signing up for a full time jailer lady. She'd probably try to outlaw sex."

"Well that's certainly the news of the day," I allowed. "No sir, no sir," Tadpole said, "that's not the number one story of the day, not by a long shot. Is it, Gus?" Gus who had made his way through the crowd nodded sagely. "You're right, Tad, that isn't the big news. The big news of this particular day is the Beaver Lady and her newly discovered bathing habits."

"Alright," I said. "What's she got to do with it? What brought about all this talk of plues and the Beaver Lady?" I asked, trying to sound like a true mountain man. "Has she gone to live in one of their lodges?"

Tad grinned, he was like his father that way, for he loved to clue you in to something he might only have heard an hour ago, but wanted to let you know he was plugged in to the town tom toms.

"Helga Merriman," he answered, a big shit-eating grin on his face, "Helga Merriman, the Beaver Lady, she's the story."

I remembered that the Beaver Lady's husband, Captain Merriman who fished George's Bank and the Flemish Cap even in winter, had had a run-in with Tad's father Pepper some years back. Some said it was over scalloping territory, others that Pepper had tried to get too friendly with Helga, but it ended up with fisticuffs over in the harbor and Pepper got a black eye. "I was just paying his wife a compliment," Pepper had claimed loudly, "you'd think he would be pleased somebody was paying the poor woman some attention what with him out to sea for weeks at a time."

Now Helga is a real fine looking woman, that's for sure. Tall, blond, with fabulous figure and carriage. She is freaking beautiful. Helga always looked like she was one of those Viking queens, who could run a whole kingdom if looks were the criterion for ruling. I'm sure more than one male in Little Harmony imagined what she looked like in the altogether. The really interesting thing was, for such a gorgeous woman, other women weren't usually jealous of her. Even Phoebe spoke highly of her and put her on a couple of library committees.

Helga was also in a lot of church and town gab fest groups and always dressed conservatively (too conservatively for many males perhaps). She never flirted or seemed to encourage the salivating, teenager like males who constantly came up to her and tried to amuse or impress her. She was happily married to the Captain, proud of his standing as the top fisherman in the area and resigned to his long absences. "It is his calling, after all," Helga said. She never seemed to encourage any of the adulation that was hers.

"I hear tell the Beaver Lady now swims in your pond, Gus, with nary a stitch on, but this I never did see. This I never did see," Tad repeated for emphasis. "Father says she has the most bodacious set of tatas in this part of the world, but I think he's just guessing. Have you seen her in your pond, Gus?"

Gus shook his head, "No. Tad, I haven't, but I admit I'd some like to—that is one fine woman. Which pond is it exactly?" Now if you had ever seen Helga in a bathing suit or shorts or a light summer dress, you would have to admit that sentiment to one and all. "Well, you should check out all your ponds around dusk." Tadpole grinned. "But I hear you can see her up by your third beaver dam. It's deep enough to swim there. Too bad you don't swim, let alone swim in fresh water. In fact, Gus, I hear tell you don't even like to get your feet wet. Too bad, she looks like a goddess in the moonlight I'm told."

Well, later when things all came to a head, I figured Gus had got to thinking about the difficulties of standing for long periods of time waiting for something that might or might not happen and what with black flies and midges and mosquitoes and all. Now normally these critters were of no consequence to Gus when he was trout fishing, let alone trout catching. But standing waiting for only the mere possible sighting of a nude Helga seemed a bit chancy, especially when it would cut into what he lovingly called his "gin time."

At the time, Gus didn't seem too interested in discussing the matter further after describing in pretty gruesome detail that disease he caught from drinking water from streams with beaver shit in them. Afterwards, I thought all that chatter was probably to throw Tadpole and I off the scent of his real plans, although we didn't grasp that at the time. Anyway, Tadpole made a grimace and moved off into the crowd heading for the Whoopie pie stand and I didn't think any more about it.

And I didn't make any connection between that conversation and Gus coming around a week or so later to borrow two of my trail cameras. I thought it odd he was setting them out so early, long before the deer season opened, what with it being July and all the leaves were out and in full foliage. Anyway, Gus seemed eager enough and who knew, I thought, he might catch that big buck whose prints we'd seen in the early spring between the second and third dam. It was one of the biggest ones I'd ever seen in Little Harmony, usually you only get a huge print like that farther north or on some big-hipped doe who'd lived to a ripe old age in town.

So it all started harmless enough: Tadpole describing the Beaver Lady swimming naked at dusk in one of his ponds and Gus getting the idea of filming her rather than standing in the gathering gloom watching her. All that could have played out nicely for him and he might well have had some first class film to amuse him on those long winter nights he used to look at deer footage.

The fly in the bug dope, as they say, turned out to be Gus's wife Willimina Sessions. A few weeks later Willimina apparently came upon Gus's trail cam footage in his study and decided to take a look at it, thinking no doubt, "No buck could be worth watching night after night." Unlike Gus who would never, ever read anybody's mail, Willimina delighted in nosing about in everybody's business and thought nothing of steaming open letters before Gus got to read them and then, assuming they were harmless, glue them back together again.

Well, she was some pissed at finding the footage of the Beaver Lady in the altogether, that's for sure. There is just no delicate way to put it, when she checked out the trail camera pointed directly at the pond and saw the Beaver Lady in all her resplendent glory. Goodness I wish I'd gotten a chance to see it, what Gus would later sadly as a terrific piece of film, with the Beaver Lady carefully and over a very long time undressing herself, washing her hair and cavorting in and out of the water without nary a beaver anywhere in sight. Although Gus later said on the tape you might have been able to hear them slapping their tails in the background if the trail cam had been wired for sound. "My God, Snappy," he said, "there's never been another woman looking like that who was interested in beavers. Of that I'm more than just sure."

Well after she saw the lengthy and by then well-watched video, Willimina commenced to get a real snoot full under her belt, using two hands with her cup of vodka no doubt. When Gus came home, there was the stomped-on trail cam lying in the driveway and his silk pj's lying right beside them. His toothbrush too.

I'll have to say, sometimes Guy can be a bit slow to read a situation with female humans, although not with game for sure. But he cottoned to this particular situation pretty quick and hence his arrival in our dooryard at dusk. "I'll head back by and by" he said, looking sheepish, "but for tonight if I could bunk in your spare room, I'd some appreciate it."

Now Willimina was surely not known for being subtle. She is some 220 pounds of hard packed muscle and she stays in great shape lifting weights and running on the treadmill every single day. She's the only person I know who thinks the NRA is a liberal bunch who compromise too much on gun issues. Willimina is fierce and will go to war at the drop of a hat or even no hat at all. She just loves to kick ass and never minds about taking names, although she does that too and those names are never just forgotten either. Willimina even cooks up coons and possum and such and Gus eats it without any fuss. She is one tough lady, for sure.

So I'm guessing Gus thought he'd actually had a narrow escape and decided to not contest the issue. We all knew Willimina was very, even extremely, territorial. She considered the 200 acres of woods around Gus's place as her domain, and she patrolled it with a vengeance.

For example, she considered every friggin' mushroom in the area her personal property and although she came down with a bad case of brown tail moth from rooting around on all fours in the leaf litter, she was still convinced every single one belonged to her. She wouldn't even tell Gus where she found the jeesly mushrooms.

When she got the chance, Willimina ruled supreme over not only Gus's land but his immediate neighbors' as well. She'd happily turf out wandering tinkers or Christmas tree tippers or sneaking-through-teenagers or anybody else crossing into that territory. But by dusk she was almost always back in her house, which is why the world lines of Helga and Willimina never crossed before that fateful day.

I'm guessing she started patrolling vigorously at sundown after checking the light on the film. Two days later Gus was allowed back home after committing totally to doing whatever penance Willimina thought appropriate—none of us ever dared to ask what that was—but we did hear about what happened to the Beaver Lady. Helga herself was some aggravated about the loud intrusion into her communion with the sunset and the beavers and didn't mind telling people at Carnot's General Store all about it.

Pepper heard it first and wasn't he all bouncy and excited about the news. He'd been paying Mistress Merriman court from time to time again despite his earlier rejections and his black eye from the Captain. Now he thought he might have a new lease on life and go down to comfort her, but Captain Merriman got back from his latest trip earlier than anticipated, and Pepper was smart enough to see the *Lady Helga* sailing into port with a full load of ground fish and decided discretion was the better part of valor although not for want of trying.

But from what Tadpole later told me, the Beaver Lady was still using Gus's third pond for her nightly cool down a couple of nights after the Fourth, not of course knowing anything about Gus's situation or what had precipitated it. So there she was at dusk, splashing and communing with the slapping tails when Willimina showed up toting that modified Armalite M-16 of hers she loves so much. She burst out onto the bank, scaring the shit out of Helga and the beavers both. Willimina aimed the sucker over Helga's head and commenced to waving it around in wild fashion. "I'm hunting plues," she announced, "but I'll settle for lesser game."

Now Helga, although usually demure, is seldom at a loss for words but I guess this was a rare time and she skedaddled out of the water some fast, picked up her clothes, and ran down the trail away from Willimina post haste. "I think the woman is pure loco," Helga told one and all later. "I hope she didn't frighten Jocko and the rest of his family. Who would ever shoot a wonderful beaver? I don't think those beavers should stay anywhere near that woman. It isn't safe. Who knows what she will do. They should all leave the area. That's what I told them to do when I went back after she'd gone to sleep that night. I told the big male Jocko to leave and take his whole family. He slapped the water four times which is our signal for 'I will.' Beavers just don't like stress and that Sessions woman is nothing but."

For her part, Willimina said when we asked her about the incident, "That woman is nutty as a fruitcake, talking to beavers, is she psychotic or what? I told her to get out and not come back. This is good news for everyone. She should be locked up if she ever comes back. I'll be seeing to that."

But for those of us hoping to have a sighting or two after we heard about her doings from Tadpole, this was not really good news and it turned out to be the end of an era.

An end of an era in more ways than one.

Still, it's an ill wind that blows no good to someone. Pepper heard soon thereafter that the Beaver Lady was now swimming down near Pollack Cove where another beaver colony was happily ensconced, whether connected to Jocko's growing brood or not. Contrary to popular opinion, plues do swim in salt water, especially when they have a good reason.

"What a fine woman," Pepper allowed, "what a christly fine woman. I think I'll check out that area. She might need some protection. There could be another jeesly Willimina down there."

Gus? Well even after he was let back into his house a few nights later, he was under something like house arrest for a full week or more. You'd call him up and ask if he wanted to go striper fishing or chumming for blue fish and he'd say quietly but firmly, "Snappy, I have a lot of chores around the house. I've been behind all summer. I need to catch up." Or, "My dooryard is stacked up with wood, I've got to move it to the shed, I'll be fishing with you guys by and by." Once he told Pepper, "A man's got to do what a man's got to do. Willimina is not a woman who forgives easily."

About the third time Gus said no, I said, "Enough said for me, he is definitely not coming out of jail anytime soon." I called Zapper and we went out and really nailed a nice bunch of stripers, but even then when I told Gus, he didn't seem that interested. He didn't even want a fish or two. "By the way," he said, "I have to buy you a new trail cam, that other one gave out. It's been hard used, for sure."

"For sure," I said. "For sure."

Ironically enough, by the next spring the beavers had all left the area. Some said it was due to the fact that they had eaten out all the poplar and alders so their food supply was gone, although they did leave behind a mess of cedars all ringed and sure to die where the young ones had tried to stay in the area but couldn't decide to keep eating just cedar bark. At least they didn't cut them all down onto the ground. In time, of course, the wind would do just that. What a fine mess they left behind.

But others believed Tadpole and Pepper when they told one and all, "It was the curse of the Beaver Lady, that's what it was. You do not want to mess with that lady, no way, no how."

For my part, I drew the same conclusion regarding Willimina.

Not that I'd ever go swimming with beavers you understand.

Unless it was in salt water maybe.

And then only if there was a proper guide around, one who knew how to communicate some good with them.

chapter
eleven

Blizzard Buck

THERE IS one thing about being a Maine Guide I don't like and I don't think I'm alone. Big Gus is not a "deer guy" because he's always more interested in partridge and geese; but for most guides, deer hunting is the big passion and it sometimes takes all the professional responsibility we can muster not to shoot the magnificent buck we are trying to put the sport in front of. Some sports deserve the shot, some don't, but your professional code doesn't allow you to distinguish, even though you often make the less deserving sport work harder for the opportunities you would eventually provide.

Still, a lot of Maine Guides feel like I do, that deer hunting is special and unless and until you got your own deer any given year, you feel unfilled. I know one year I didn't get "my deer" and I felt distressed for a whole year thereafter. Maybe that year I didn't deserve to get it.

Anyway, there is an old Maine country saying that asserts "It's better to be lucky than good when it comes to love and deer hunting." Now I know that people who watch today's Outdoor Channel and *The Bone Collectors* would be prepared to throw that old saw on the ash heap of history what with trail cams and GPS and range finders and scent blocker dispensers, feed machines and the like. They've seen on TV deer hunts where the critters are monitored from year to year until they are just right to be "harvested" on camera on a given day and I'm sure viewers think it's more science than art. And there are a lot of nimrods who think it is all about their skill in the woods.

But deer hunting has a lot of luck in it, no matter how good you think you are or how good you really are. You can cut down the odds with scouting and experience and hard work, but at the end of the day, Gus and I always said we would trade skill for luck any day when it comes to deer hunting. That and timely information. The kind where the farmer says, "I just came from the pine grove. That buck is going to wear himself out today servicing those three does. He's in a real foolish mood." That kind of stuff is what others today call "actionable."

My grandson Dusty was asking me the other day what was my most exciting buck and he said, "Snappy, you have a lot of deer pictures on the wall and you've helped others get their deer heads on their walls, but which one meant the most to you?"

I thought about it for quite a while looking over the pictures on the wall and I had to admit it was "the blizzard buck." Then I also had to spend a lot of time explaining to his five-year-old mind what "serendipity" really is all about. The blizzard buck wasn't my biggest or most deserving or most "I've figured out the white tail deer thing" buck, but it was the most amazing. By far.

It started innocently enough. My wife Sunny and I were at a party and about to head home around midnight as it had begun snowing big time. I was complaining how poor the deer hunting had been that fall and how I was hoping the snow would change things. My neighbor Tommy, one of the original "coulda, shoulda, woulda" guys, overheard my lament and said, "Roli saw five deer on the tip of Dockery Island, right up by the old graves. You should try there, Snappy."

Well I knew that place very well as I'd often stood on that point during bird hunting or deer expeditions and pondered the overgrown gravesite on that spot. The very weathered and leaning gravestone says it commemorates a seventeen-year-old girl who had died in 1807. It doesn't say from what she died, but for some reason I always thought it was pneumonia in the middle of the winter. It's a poignant reminder how lucky we are to live when we do.

Anyway, that night it snowed and snowed and snowed. I could hardly close my eyes. I was so excited about the deer on the point of the island and the brand new tracking snow. I knew the deer wouldn't be feeding in the middle of the blizzard so at dawn, or whenever the blizzard stopped, they would be very hungry and moving a lot. Every time I got up to look, the snow was coming sideways and the wind howled. "What an old-fashioned blizzard," I thought. If I could just get to that peninsula right after dawn, I could catch them coming out to feed. I got more and more excited just thinking about it and hardly slept after that.

About dawn the wind shifted to the northwest. By the time I left the dock and rowed across to the island, the snow had stopped. There must have been nine or ten inches on the ground as I pressed inland, hell bent for the tip of the island. I had to get there quickly.

That's when my troubles began.

The island was covered in a mantel of white. It was like hunting in one of those snow globes, white everywhere and with the howling of the wind and the muffling impact of the snow, you could move silently through the woods. It was like being in an enchanted world.

Now the wind was blowing the snow off the trees at a rapid rate and it fell in big hunks on my head and shoulders and the piled up snow fell into my boots. I paid no attention at first, I was so excited and so anxious to get to the old grave-yard and shoot a deer I just pushed head, hell bent for leather.

On and on I trudged, for perhaps a mile at least, certain I was going to get there ahead of anybody else and get a deer. Everything looked like it was swathed in white cotton candy. Several times I thought I saw a deer bedded down in the swamp but then I remembered the local legend Wayne the Tree Killer and I didn't want to mistake a stump and branches for a deer bedded down and looking up. I would take a second look through the scope and then push on.

I got wetter and wetter as the snow kept dropping on me. Finally, my boots came undone and I had to sit down and get squared away. I found a log out of the wind and sat down, putting my gun upright but out of reach.

As I tried to empty my boots of the accumulated snow and then retie them, I thought, "What if a deer comes by while my rifle is out of reach?" And then I thought, "Well, you've sat down a thousand times in the woods taking a break (as opposed to choosing a stand and waiting for the deer to come by) and only once had a deer ever come by when you were sitting. Still, I felt uneasy and got up and put my gun beside me before returning to fix my boots.

Just then I heard a thrashing, smashing sound. It was a buck marking his territory, using his antlers to knock over small saplings and leave rub marks on the bigger trees. My heart started beating like a drum. The woods were very thick and he was coming right across my front but there was only a tiny opening where I could see even a fraction of him. The entire scene was bathed in white.

Then I saw his antlers. "At least eight points" I gasped. Then his body moved into the tiny frame. There was his shoulder. I raised my .44 magnum ("The perfect brush gun for cedar swamps" the folks at L.L.Bean had once pronounced and I believe them, it is just right for the thick, deep Maine woods). It *is* great brush gun, good at short range with lots of stopping power. I didn't think much as just swung it into the sight pattern. "Wump" went the gun as even the report was muffled by the snow. The deer fell down instantly. I'd shot him right through the shoulder and into the heart. He was dead by the time I got over to him.

Even now I can feel that thrill, the sense of wonder and accomplishment. There I was, so early in the morning, a beautiful season-validating buck down and all mine and all accomplished because of good intelligence and hard work and the gift of a blizzard. Meat for the family all winter long.

I was so happy and fulfilled. What a gift!

I quickly cleaned the deer, carefully wrapping the liver and heart in a plastic bag, already tasting the night's dinner (this, of course was long before we realized the toxic residues in the liver of wild creatures and stopped thinking of them as delicacies). I put my rope around the deer's neck and with a burst of energy started dragging him back to the boat.

I was euphoric.

I pressed on, snow falling from the limbs, across a rise and down into the middle of the island swamp and across the swamp. It was like Alice in Wonderland. I was propelled by happiness and sense of achievement. Unmindful of direction or being soaked by the snow or aching muscles.

Finally I saw the sea between the trees. I had made it to the shore. Home was right across the bay. What an accomplishment. Then I saw the sun through the clouds. I was deflated. Horrified. "Holy Christ, what an idiot you are, Snappy," I said to myself, "the sun is in the wrong frigging place." Somehow, my adrenal and failure to check my compass even once had propelled me across the island in the wrong direction. What a mess. I was deflated, exhausted, and over a mile or more from my boat. Some atavistic worry surfaced. Someone would take my deer from me if I didn't get to my boat. I had to get out of there, I had to get home.

I finally broke down and took a quick reading on my compass saying to myself, "Duh, you're a Maine Guide, act like one." I realized I had gone in the exact opposite direction. Taking some deep breaths, I started dragging the deer to the west. Back across the high ground. Back into the cedar swamp. Back towards the far shore. Like a man possessed. Which I suppose I was.

I dragged and dragged for an eternity before I saw the shore. There was my boat. I was home free. Or almost. I loaded the deer in the bow of the tin boat and pushed out into the teeth of a thirty or forty mph northwest wind. I could see my house. I was almost there. I rowed like a madman.

But it soon dawned on me that I was already exhausted. The wind was blowing the boat south faster than I could row it west and the magnificent deer was dead weight. It was disturbing to say the least. I redoubled my efforts but lost ground with every oar stoke (and more when I rested). I had visions of being swept out to sea. Also, I had been sweating like a stuck pig all across the swamp, but now that I was out in the freezing wind, I felt incredibly cold. I was losing muscle control along with my judgment.

My house was rapidly receding to the north. So were the houses of my neighbors. Soon they would be out of sight. I was only halfway across the sound and getting weaker by the minute. I don't know how I rowed that last half mile and when I finally hit the shore I was more than a half mile from my house. Luckily it was low tide so I could beach the boat and drag it along the shore. I could see my house in the distance and I had my treasure but I literally did not know how I was going to reach home safely.

Luckily, Sunny had been watching my struggles and being swept down the bay. She called Big Gus and then she rushed down to the shore to help me. I was on my hands and knees on the seaweed, dragging the boat with the buck a yard at a time along the shore into the wind.

Now there have been some magic moments when I saw Sunny. The first was when she came out of the surf at Popham

Beach and time stopped for me. Then there was the time I took her to the prom. And of course the times our children were born and I first saw them in her arms were very special. But if I'm being truly honest, she was never a more welcome sight when she showed up while I was down on my knees in the seaweed, holding on to that boat with the buck in it.

"My God, you look like you're about to pass out," Sunny said as she began to pull the boat herself up against the wind and the tide. Together, but with her doing most of the work, we dragged the boat against the wind and finally made it back to the mooring. By the time Gus arrived we were back at the haul-off and he was able to help us tie the boat up and drag the deer up the bank. He then helped us hang it from our barn.

"Nice buck," he said laconically. "You can tell me about it later. I have a meeting in town" was all he said.

But by the time he got back from town, I had gone into full hibernation. I sat in front of the fire and ate some breakfast and fell into a deep, deep sleep, dreaming of deer liver and bacon and that special Jack Daniel's Sunny had been saving for a special occasion. Big Gus, no doubt would have a Chateau Neuf du Pape with his tenderloin when I gave him some. What a sense of relief and accomplishment and well-being washed over me. I must have slept right through the day because it was almost dark when I woke up.

"Tommy's here, admiring your deer," my Sunny told me so I went out into the cold evening air and looked at my hanging buck with awe and reverence and feeling pretty damn good about things.

My neighbor stood there nodding. "I see you finally got your buck."

"Well, it was all thanks to you, Tommy. If you hadn't told me last night about the lobsterman seeing all those deer on the point, I'd never have gone out in that gale, I can tell you. Thanks a million. You made my season. I really appreciate it."

Tommy looked at me oddly, almost as if I was mentally unbalanced. Then he shook his head sadly. "For crumb's sake bud." He laughed out loud. "That was last August he seen those deer."

For sure in deer hunting, as in love, it truly is better to be lucky than good.

As Gus put it later, "Snap, it isn't the reliability of the report, it's believing the report. You always hunt different knowing you've got some true gen info, even if that true info is punk rotten."

Another truth from Big Gus recorded.

chapter twelve

Big Gus Shoots
with the Queen

"**ISN'T THAT** Uncle Gus on the wall?" Stevie asked when he saw the picture of Big Gus on the wall of Andre's Rod and Gun Shop. "It sure looks like him." My grandsons Stevie and his brother Guido were up from D.C. for a vacation and I'd taken them to Andre's to get them some pin-on compasses so they could learn about directions when I took them out in the woods. For some reason that fall, those little pin-ons were some hard to come by and Andre had just called to let me know he got a shipment in.

Now Andre is only about five-foot-two and that's in his black combat boots which he wears all the time. Andre may be a tad short, but he wears a Coonan .357 magnum 1911 high on his hip and swaggers around as if he were much taller, hence his strange moniker I guess. But they call him Andre the Giant and Andre the Giant is what he is. He fills up any room, waving his arms and talking like he has a bull horn in his hand.

Andre's bait, ammo, and tackle shop is pretty typical of that type of establishment all over the State of Maine. Tons of gear, lures, calls, guns, rods, coolers, maps, you name it. Now not all of this stock is totally useful, of course, but that gear always sold with a maximum amount of authority.

"You will, never, ever find a better knife than this one. It's tough plastic, it sure is. Space age plastic, really tough," Andre will declare. Or let's say you want a fresh water lure and see a pile of them and Andre spies you looking at them. "Those lures are massively good on bass. I tell you a fella could catch a bushel of bass with one or two of those for sure."

And when the sport says, "Actually I was looking for something for pickerel." Well, Andre would never miss a beat; he'd gesture even more wildly and burst out "Pickerel? Pickerel? These spoons was *made* for pickerel. The bass just happen to like them too. You can't go wrong with Grandma Weider's Golden Spoon lures of any type or dimension, I tell you that."

And so it goes. Hour by hour. Day by day. Except for Christmas, Andre's Gun and Tackle Shop is open for business all year-round. I honestly don't know when he sleeps.

And Giant, as Pepper insists on calling him, always knows just where the fish and game are.

Or, more precisely, where they were.

"They was slaying them over in the New Meadows yesterday," he'd assure the sport or "I guess they got into them some good Tuesday off Gun Point." "Oh my gosh you should have been over in Jones's Eel's Eddy last weekend. The stripers were real thick." "Last night we had some skin-diver's out down in Lowell's Cove; they saw a ton, a ton of bluefish. Up close too."

Now, Andre hardly ever has any information from that particular day however. That's in part because neither Andre nor his partner, Two Tone Cutone, ever hunts or fishes. They just rely on super good tales by and for sports and other assorted pigeons as they drift through the shop. One time Cutone was taken smelt fishing by one of the locals to show him how it's done when dipping at night. But in the gloom,

Cutone's white strip of hair earned him the name "Two Tone" and he never went back. He did tell Andre, though, that "Two Tone" was better than being called "Skunky."

Also, like many other firearms emporiums, there are several "Protected by Smith & Wesson" signs prominently displayed. All feature a picture of an enormous gun pointed right at you. Those posters freaked my grandsons out the first time they saw them, for sure. "Those are really scary Snappy."

Of course, as Pepper often says, "Those Smith and Wessons may be well made and even well trained and some could even be good on malfactors, but it would take them guns a christly long time to crawl out of their locked cases if they was ever needed in an emergency. Giant would have to rely on his big Coonan, that is, of course, if he could ever get the jeesly thing out of that holster rig he's got when he needed it. I tell you my money would be on the robbers."

It actually *was* a picture of Gus, right up there on the wall, framed and all and looking for all the world like a young Ernest Hemingway. An important *New York Times* outdoor writer had heard about Gus (and his dogs) prowess on grouse and woodcock and had come up to Maine just to check him out. The writer had enjoyed a fabulous hunt, shot his limit of woodcock and grouse in the special covers Gus took him to and as thanks, gave Gus his due in print. It was a great story up there on the wall and with that terrific picture that Andre, who never missed an opportunity to promote his shop, had framed and put up right there beside his prized Smith & Wesson posters.

Not that Big Gus wasn't a good deer hunter as well. He was sure pretty good at that. But he did prefer birds, ruffed grouse especially and woodcock, and he almost always had a pair of hanging on the shady side of his porch during the bird season. He was good at it, plain and simple good at it. And relentless to boot.

Gus was also one of the few Maine Guides who had, as he was fond of saying, "shot with the Queen." Perhaps "with" is stretching it a bit because the Queen was shooting a couple of glens over that time he went to Scotland. I know because I was with him, thanks to his generosity. If you looked real close, you could see Balmoral Castle way off in the distance a couple of glens away, but it was the size of an ant castle.

Still, that was pretty close after all, for two shit kickers from Maine. And for a Maine Guide of Gus's predilection, it was pretty close to perfection hunting in those highlands, staying in that sprawling manor house and walking up grouse in the heather while listening to the Queen and the Duke blast away in that nearby glen. What a fusillade came from Balmoral that day. We calculated they took one hundred shots to every one for our party. The Queen's husband, the Duke, himself must have shot two hundred birds on his own that Glorious Twelfth day of August.

How did that happen? Well after being chosen "Maine Guide of the Year" and getting that nice and well deserved write-up in the *New York Times*, Gus was selected by the Maine Fish and Game Department to represent THE GREAT STATE OF MAINE at an Edinburgh, Scotland, conference on game management.

I remember there were many seminars on feeding and protecting and otherwise managing the red grouse population. As near as I could figure out, the management considered pretty much of wiping out every possible predator from foxes to rats to crows to stroats and, if nobody was looking, eagles and harriers of all stripe and size.

Reminded me a little of Maine hunters bound and determined to eliminate coyotes so as to prevent coyotes from getting "their deer." But those game keepers in the British Isles were even more relentless, relentless against all those predators, animal, avian, and human. Made for some good shooting, though, all that care and feeding and protection of the grouse. They even burned the heather of the upland moors in patches and strips to ensure fresh heather shoots for the birds.

With nobody else to cancel them out during the year, there sure were a lot of red grouse scooting and flying around on the Glorious Twelfth of August when the season on red grouse opened. At the conference they said that almost 50 percent of that season's birds would die naturally, so it was best to harvest them with guns before that happened. And doing it during the first few days gave you the best chance, rather like our handling of the excess pheasant population.

Anyway, Gus was kind enough to invite my wife Sunny and me along, even though he knew my outdoor garb (especially my baseball hat) would be an embarrassment to him. Gus, on the other hand, looked so much like he belonged on the heather that the head gamekeeper and the lord of the manor both automatically treated him as the leader of our little group.

Gus did look like he had been to the manor born and would have easily fitted in to any type of English or Scottish hunt what with his tweeds and one of those funny looking Sherlock Holmes caps. Even though the laird looked down on our using .16-gauge shotguns ("It's most unsual to use those. Most would think you under-gunned"), the fact that Gus was carrying a Purdy got him cut some slack.

The laird himself didn't much like foreigners to begin with so the two pushy French guys and one young Belgian fellow shooting with us especially grated on him some fierce. So did I, but the laird and the gamekeeper liked Sunny from the first. "She's a comely lass and not afraid of walking," McIvor the Head Gamekeeper had offered after the first day. "And her name is most fitting for such a lass. She's a happy figure walking the heather. Always smiling, even in the rain and mist."

They agreed also that Big Gus belonged in Scotland for he was one of their own (and probably had been in an earlier life) and, of course, his Purdy was noticed by one and all as well. In fact, the laird was so interested in it that before we boarded the plane for home, I urged Gus to make sure the laird hadn't switched guns on him. What with the death duties and all, I thought the laird was some hard up for cash, if not why have us yahoos marauding around on his estate if not for the cash?

"I say," the laird said more than once to me, "do you American chaps always dress that way when going afield?" I looked down on my yellow slicker pullover and allowed as how I did anyway. Gus had said he would be mortified if I brought my Stevens along, despite its good track record, so he lent me his beautiful little 16-gauge Bernadelli with superb scrollwork which he called "Young Bernadelli." Now Young Bernadelli, as dependable and fully choked as it was, turned out to be great for those long, quartering away shots the grouse often gave you. The lord looked down on that too, however, as being "Eye talion" and hence a cut below standards, even as he briefly admired the scroll work on it. And he was totally amazed that "a Colonial" like Gus could drive a Land Rover. "They sell them in America, what?"

Excited as we were, we got up early for breakfast. That was when I made my first big mistake. You know all the parts of the deer we cut out and throw away? Well I swear the Scots take those parts and grind them all up and make sausage out of them. They then commence to serve a breakfast called "The Full House," which is a ton of sausages, eggs, bacon, other pieces of meat, oatmeal, toast, and so on. These "Full Houses" tasted great but were cooked in lard fat. Long story short, they are not, at least not in terms of their impact on digestive systems not used to them, a good idea before a long hunt up and down the heather when on foot. They sit in your stomach in a huge lump and you trudge along like you had a ten-pound weight in your gut.

Sunny wisely ate only the oatmeal and she bounced along with great vigor. So when I complained, she said, "Scotland one, Snappy zero." She hiked along with the line and was happy as a clam. But that night when we ate the grouse, Scotland got its revenge on her. At home, we hang the birds a couple of days, but only after carefully cleaning them and scrubbing the stomach cavity squeaky clean. Sunny eats the whole bird, crushing the bones with the gusto of some long gone cave woman.

Well she tried that with the Scots grouse and ended up eating feathers and some offal. When the laird heard she ate the bones, he was non-plussed, "You mean she actually grinds up the bones with her teeth? Those Americans are a strange breed." Sunny was up and down to the bathroom all night long. Scotland two, Adams family zero.

The first day, it was clear Gus was in his element as we walked up on the grouse. He shot the first bird neatly, a quartering away shot, low and chancy. Then he hit another after one of the French lads missed it. Gus was on a roll and in a role. He was born for this, Sunny and I could tell.

The keeper had arranged the line of guns with a beater and dog at either end. Gus and the gamekeeper McIvor in the middle and the Frenchies and Belgian out on one wing and me on the other. Sunny followed behind because she was concerned about being in the way and getting shot. But McIvor kept telling her, "Close up, lassie, close up," thinking it was more dangerous to be lagging behind.

For my part, I started off horribly, missing the first three birds which rose from the heather. The light bothered me. The lack of trees bothered me. The scale seemed all wrong. The grouse seemed smaller than ours in Maine and they flew different. Plus there were distractions. We actually could see Balmoral Castle off in the far distance, several glens away. And hear it all day long. It sounded like Gettysburg or Anzio or Normandy, tremendous fusillades rolling and reverberating over and over again.

"They must have thousands of birds over there," one of the French guys complained, "beaucoup more than we have." "At the very least," McIvor answered, as if pleased at the state of affairs. "She is the Queen, after all, at least to some laddies."

I also couldn't seem to get used to the way the grouse burst up and away, not rising high like a pheasant or American grouse, but flying close to the ground like they had ground hugging radar. By the third miss, I was spooked. Even the Belgian young guy was dropping birds and I was here doing nothing and in front of Sunny to boot. Then I remembered the words of Old Rope, "If it has feathers or fur on it, you can hit it."

Soon afterwards, there arose a huge clatter behind me and to my right. Out of a big gully rose the biggest, blackest grouse I'd ever seen. It was a difficult shot but I took it anyway as the dog handlers and McIvor yelled, "Black Game, Black Game." I thought sure that was a prize. Boom. The Black Game dropped instantly. What a shot. I turned to receive what I thought would be the praise of my fellow gunners. But instead one of the dog handlers yelled, "Prohibited Game. Prohibited Game."

Huh? How could that be? Now I felt really bad and hung my head, thinking that would be the end of my gunning on the heath. How was I to know the season for Black Game wasn't for another couple of weeks? But as the dog man came by to retrieve the black game he grinned, "You'll be owing McIvor a bottle of the best, in fact, I'd make it two if you want to hunt on the morrow. He'll dispose of this tonight for you."

Well, I could do that at least. And all the ruckus seemed to loosen me up and I began to shoot better. Everybody bagged a few birds and the dogs worked well. We took a break at one point and McIvor pointed to a far ridge. "See that stag?"

Way off in the distance there was big red stag. It must have been a mile away, outlined against the sky. What a magnificent sight. A glorious creature almost like in a picture book of the highlands. "If the people in Maine could only see us now," I thought. "This is a magic moment."

Especially if Pepper could see us, I imagined, he'd be thinking how to get us back out here in the moonlight for a stalk and how to get a light up on that ridge. For his part, Little Robert would like to have put one of the blue ticks on the track and never worry if he ever saw the stag again. He'd just listen to the music as the dogs chased the stag for a great distance. And with so few trees, the music would really carry from glen to glen.

But Zapper? Seeing that stag which the keeper said cost five thousand quid to shoot, well, Zapper would have taken a shot on the stag outlined on that hill no matter how far away it was. Zapper always said, "If you don't shoot at it, you can't hit it." He'd take the shot alright come hell or high water. But he wouldn't pay the fee even if he got the stag, I know that much.

Then the line moved forward again and we began to shoot even better and by the end of the day Gus and I were pretty happy. No, I was pretty happy, Gus was ecstatic. It was pretty cool to come back to the manor and have servants take our guns to be cleaned and our L.L.Bean boots to be cleaned. This had never happened to any Maine Guide I ever heard about at least. I'd never known of anyone except the guide cleaning the mud off his boots. Sunny said it was like living in "Upstairs, Downstairs," at least for a while although the butler wasn't as welcoming as Hudson.

"This is the life," Gus said, "this is a little bit of the alright." "A little bit of the alright" is his phrase for "Really Terrific."

But over dinner, the French guys and the Belgian pup, Marcusa I think his name was, complained as to how few birds we'd seen compared to other shoots he'd been on over on the Continent, and he was convinced that we'd stopped too soon that day.

When they brought this to the attention of the laird and he then communicated these sentiments to McIvor (who was at that very moment no doubt feasting on the Black Game and consoling himself with more than one dram of Scotch) McIvor became quite irate, telling the lord, "First day hunt. With a lassie, no need to overdo it I thought. Those lads want to have more action, they'll have more action tomorrow. I promise you that." Then McIvor called the manor and left us a message he would come for us right after breakfast.

"Oh God," I thought, "we'll be hiking up and down and down and up until we collapse." Unfortunately, I was right. McIvor set off at a rapid clip first thing the next morning. We must have done five miles up and down the glens before lunch. I was exhausted, although Sunny still looked chipper and Gus was still in Maine Guide in Holiday Heaven mode. That's when I took it upon myself to throw the complainers under the bus. Gus was too much of a gentleman to do it, so I took McIvor aside and, giving him the second bottle of Scotch said, "I don't think it was right for those foreigners to complain. They even bitched about the wine last night." McIvor brightened up. "That is right, lad. That is right. They were never any good at all, haven't been since before Boney tried to beat us down. I'm glad you know it."

Mercifully after lunch the pace slowed down, at least for some of us.

McIvor grinned as he rearranged the gun line. I was next to the left beater. Gus was next to me. Then came McIvor, then the Belgian kid and the two Frenchies on the right end with the other beater. Sunny was right behind Gus. She can smell a winner from miles away and he was the gun with the hot hand.

"We'll be picking up the pace, gentlemen," said McIvor even before we'd finished the last of the tea. "We have a lot of ground to cover. Up and at them then, lads, there's some good fellows."

Now McIvor obviously knew every nook and cranny of the entire estate. And he now had complete control over the miscreants who had spoiled his peaceful dinner and dram. So in what Gus and I remember as a series of pinwheel maneuvers, he kept the gun line moving continuously forward, but always swinging to the left so the Belgian kid and the Frenchies had to walk twice, even three times as far as Gus, Sunny, and me, not to mention McIvor.

The French guys and Belgian kid really had to pick up the pace just to stay even. The shooting was pretty consistent but it always seemed that most the birds came out of the gullies, to the left and across the line of guns so Gus and I had first crack at them. Only if both of us missed did they get a shot, and we had a hot hand that afternoon, firing on all cylinders.

This fast pace continued on for over an hour, punctuated by a most amusing episode. The Belgian guy disappeared on one of the wheel-abouts and soon we heard a strangled cry, "Help. Help. Help me." From the pitch of his voice we couldn't tell whether it was fear, excitement, or desire. We all looked right and McIvor took a couple of steps in that direction. "What's up, laddie?" he called out. "Come. Come," the kid answered. We came over a rise and looked down into the bottom of the gully. There was a sheep, mired in a big mud wallow up to its shoulders with the Belgian kid trying to pull him out by his head. The French guys stood nearby, nonplussed. "Well don't just stand there, laddies, help him out. You chaps from the Continent, be of use."

Then, as Sunny, Gus, and I watched, the Frenchmen and the Belgian kid pushed and prodded and pulled to get the sheep out of the mud hole. Of course they got soaked and mud spattered in the process. Once the sheep was free and its bleating less alarming, McIvor blew his whistle. "Off we go then."

The Continental lads looked dazed.

Off we did go. Up and down we went, again the gun line still wheeling ever to the left. The Frenchies and the Belgian guy, wet, mud coated, and now very tired, had to constantly move to catch up. In this dazed condition, they missed a lot of shots to boot.

Then the high point of the hunt, at least for some, occurred.

For some reason, no birds had flushed directly back over the gun line all day. Now, suddenly, two red grouse burst out of the heather and over the head of Gus. They were the only birds to do so that day. Gus took the first with one barrel and then the second over his shoulder even as it got behind the gun line. The entire line of guns and the two dog handlers turned along with McIvor, and someone shouted, "Well played." It was a hell of a double. And even McIvor grinned and for once added, "Fine shot that." Both birds sailed toward the ground.

Well right before this strange but marvelous turn of events, Sunny had gotten a call of nature. Silently and unobtrusively, she'd dropped back and hiked up her skirt and squatted in the heather to attend to her business. "Goodness," she thought, "peace at last." But then the shouts and the shots commenced.

Both birds sailed earthward, nearly bracketing her. One bird flew over her head and dropped behind her, the other landed right beside her. Looking surprised but nonplussed, she still smiled as the birds arrived expectantly.

Bad luck there as the entire line now turned to watch the dogs retrieve the two fallen birds around her. Everybody stopped and watched one of the most unusual of sights to be seen that season on the heather of Loc McIntyre. Even the dogs turned and bounded toward her. She was the center of attention. The true center of attention.

Things looked a tad awkward.

But then, asserting his best keeper, "I'm in charge here" voice, McIvor took things firmly in hand and called out, "All right, laddies, steady as you go. Eyes forward. Move the line along smartly. No dawdling. Give the lassie some privacy if you please. There are birds coming up."

"That's a good lad," he added, prodding the youngest of the Frenchies with his walking stick. "You too. They'll be no more complaints about the laird's wine tonight."

And there wasn't.

The Continental chaps were nearly asleep by the soup course.

chapter thirteen

Willimina Kicks Serious Butt

I **WENT INTO** Andre's Bait and Tackle shop the other day to get some and there were Zapper and Little Robert standing with Andre the Giant while Big Gus was waving around a piece of paper with a vengeance and talking up a storm.

As I came closer, Gus was holding the paper tight in his big paw and repeating, obviously for my benefit since I'd missed the early part of the conversation, "Guys, I'm some proud of Willimina, guys, some proud of her indeed. Look at this. The Commissioner himself came down and delivered her this letter yesterday. He was apologizing for that damn warden Pinch. He even tore up the tickets and handed them to her, telling her to put them in her scrapbook. She was tickled pink, I've never seen her so happy. She's a hell of a woman, I'd much rather see her happy than on the warpath."

Willimina's run-in with Warden Charles Pinch had been the talk of the town for months after he gave her a summons for fishing in a closed lake upcountry by Milo. Among her many local activities, Willimina heads up the local Girl Scout troop in the area and she and Zapper always take them ice fishing in the winter. "These kids need to get outside and get some real exercise, get toughened up, you know what I mean?" she is fond of saying.

And not only the Girl Scouts get horsed along on these ventures. The Boy Scouts go as well, although lawyer Basil Thompson, the scoutmaster, is not exactly a poster boy for the out of doors. He's more into sitting by the fire and having the lads tie knots or do crafts or some such indoor activity. He's a good old soul, however, and is useful for toning down Willimina, at least on occasion. Gus once asked him about taking the scouts on some "hardship" winter camping and he said with a knowing grin, "For me, Gus, a hardship is the power going out and me not having enough chips."

Gus and I have never been invited on one of these rambles; we think Willimina likes to be in charge. Hell, we know Willimina likes to be in charge. But she has enough sense to hook up with an up-country guide, usually Brad Pelt who specializes in the lake country north of Bangor. But this year Brad was tied up. He did tell her the ice was safe and that his sports had been limiting out so she was encouraged. "We'll do fine," she said, "I can take it from here, Brad, as you well know."

Anyway, this past January, Willimina and Bill Thompson and one set of parents, Bill and Carol McNamara, took the scouts, about a dozen in all, up country to a sporting camp near Milo where they all stayed together. Zapper also went as he usually does. He provides the bait and is always good with kids, telling them stories of his adventures out in the woods and on the water. Most years they try to stay with Hiram and Peggy Clinton who run the Pucker Brush Camps.

The trip got off to a great start. Three hour ride passed quickly as the caravan of trucks and cars headed north and the kids were impressed with the sight of the Great North Woods getting denser and denser. The camps all had fires blazing in them when they arrived and soon it was time for dinner. Peggy always pushed the wild game on the scouts saying, "People eat too much store bought, dontcha know." So she served them venison and baked potatoes and smelts and homemade biscuits. I'm not sure the kids would have eaten rhubarb at home, but up there they tucked into it some good that night according to Zapper. He added it was a good thing Willimina hadn't brought any of her possum and turnip soup. "Peggy would have drawn the line at that."

After dinner, the kids played card games with Hiram, the McNamaras, and Peggy while Zappy and Willimina and Bill sat around and poured over the map and Maine's fishing rule book. That latter tome requires a lot of close study. It will make your head hurt, I guarantee that. A man needs a couple of drinks just to start tackling it. There are rules about rules—four pages alone on the Kennebec River—telling you what fish you can take where, what ponds and lakes are open for which fish and how many can be taken when and where and went and so on. They carefully checked the list of ponds and lakes closed to fishing in Piscataquis County.

Then commenced some serious disagreement.

Willimina wanted everybody to go deep bushwhacking before they started fishing so she kept choosing ponds or lakes well back from the road. "I want to get them tuckered out before we drill the holes," she said. "I want them unstarched and none too overeager." But Zapper and Bill, more sensible, said the snowshoeing a long way through the woods with scouts straggling far and wide might be a tad rough to police so they picked Perch Pond which was close to the road and not too far from the camp.

Willimina only sulked a little while after being outvoted.

She did recover her good humor when she told the scouts her good night story, however. Several years back she had taken a mixed group of scouts over in New Hampshire and in the middle of the night a big black bear sow came into camp and started to root around for grub. Willimina yelled like a demon and raced out to the fire, picking up a flaming brand and smacking the bear along the side of the head with it. Startled and confused by a human her own size, the sow barreled off, no doubt thinking, "This ain't a very hospitable camp site, I'd do well to avoid it in the future."

Several scouts got a bit nervous and asked, "Will there be bears out on the ice?" Zapper and Bill assured them they wouldn't, although Willimina was a bit cagy. "You never know what can happen in the out of doors. That's why our motto is 'Always be Prepared.'" "I don't want to be prepared for no bear," said Warren Whitehouse, the oldest of the scouts. "Bears grabbing at your butt hole in the middle of the night is not, cannot, and will not be my idea of fun."

Willa passed right over his concerns and the fact that all the bears were actually in hibernation. "Anyway you've got me and bears are afraid of me." Zapper told me later he had a hard time not adding, "And a ton of humans are too," but being a man of few words, he thought better of it.

Zapper did add his own bit to the night terror of the scouts however. As the fire died down, he told all the scouts to look carefully into it. "We are not far from Stanley Gore, kids, it's a few miles northeast of here. In that there Gore is Willoby Woods, a real thick patch of very tall pines. It's a very mysterious place."

Then in a low, menacing voice he recited over and over a short rhyme from his childhood "There once was a witch from Willowby Woods," he intoned, "and a real wild witch was she. She could jump to the moon and back, but this I never did see. This I never did see."

Looking furtively around and making it seem like the only reason he didn't see the witch was because he was looking in the wrong direction, Zapper repeated it several more times until one scout let out a cry, "I do not want to hear any more about witches, we are in the godforsaken big woods for cripes sake. Who knows what is out there?"

Between images of marauding bears and wild witches, to say nothing of the excitement of being in the Great North Woods for the first time, few of the scouts, male or female, got much sleep that night. Little did they know their night terrors would only grow on the morrow.

The next morning after a big hunter's breakfast with all kinds of fried sausage and bacon and even some moose steaks along with blueberry pancakes and home fries and muffins and toast, the group headed out, reaching Perch Pond a little before 10 a.m. The sun was shining and they got all ready to fish. The scouts helped with the setting up of the tips after Zapper bored the holes. Then they threw snowballs at one another. Willimina joined in and beaned a couple of boy scouts while gesturing to the girls, "That's how it's done." The boy scouts shortly commenced going back to helping Zapper with the tip ups. Even Bill was subdued. "How she ever got to lead a Girl Scout troop, I will never know."

Action began right away. Several Girl Scouts shrieked when the first flag went up and Zapper let the one who spotted it first pull in the fish. It was a nice 10-inch brookie so into the cooler it went. The next hour or so passed quickly and pleasantly. The action was pretty steady and by noon the scouts had amassed nine or ten brook trout, one of them over a foot long. Everybody was pleased and Zapper nodded his head in satisfaction. "You bunch of pups be golldern good fishermen." "We're from the coast. We're from the coast" went up the chant. "We are from the coast and we will beat the dung-eyes farmers hollow every time."

Zapper smiled tolerantly at that. He was used to island and coastal folks coming inland and thinking themselves pretty darn good overall, and with fishing specifically, so it was no surprise that his younger generation had a fine, high opinion of their fishing prowess. "You are all planning to be highliners, I can tell." He grinned and they all nodded. "Yes sir, we are. Yes sir, we sure are."

Next thing you known along comes a snowmobile barreling toward them along the ice. It turned out to be a warden. As soon as the warden stopped, Bill went right over and introduced himself. "I'm Bill Thompson, I'm the scoutmaster. We're up here doing a little fishing." Not to be outdone, Willimina pushed ahead of him and said, "The Girl Scouts caught most of the fish and I'm their leader. I'm in charge of the whole shebang. Nice to meet you. What can we do for you? Just dropped by to check out our catch, I'll bet. We're well within the limit."

"Well," said the warden with a grin. "I don't know about that. For the record, my name is Charles Pinch and all you folks are in a lot of trouble."

"What trouble?" bellowed Willimina, "what trouble? We did everything by the book. Bag limit. Size limit. Every damn thing."

"Not everything, lady, not everything." Pinch smirked, obviously enjoying the whole encounter. "This pond is closed to ice fishing." Now if there's one thing that sets Willimina off is to be referred to as a "lady." "Hell," she is fond of saying, "I'm no lady, I'm as tough as any man and twice as smart." Her face got very red as she started to hyperventilate.

"What the hell are you talking about?" she retorted. "Bill, get me the rule book. I'll show this yahoo we're legal."

The warden's grin got even wider as Bill got the rule book out of his pack and nervously began thumbing through it trying to find the proper section. The Warden tipped his hat back as Bill fumbled and fumbled until he found it. "Here, officer, right here. Here's the list of waters closed to ice fishing. Perch Pond is not on it."

"Well that's where the lady and you are all wrong. That's a list of waters that are open to ice fishing. I say again 'Open to Ice Fishing.' The rest of the water in this county are closed, closed to ice fishing and that includes this here Perch Pond.

I've got you good and proper for fishing on a closed water and for ten fish over your limit which for the limit is zero. Shame on you two for making these scouts break the law. You grown-ups should be ashamed of yourselves. You lady most of all, you being the leader as you said. Leader of a bunch of outlaws, that's what I make it."

Willimina lost it about there. She charged toward the warden and only Zapper and Bill restraining her prevented more serious charges from being filed.

Bill tried to head off the coming fiasco. "Wait a minute, officer. Please, I'm an attorney down in Cumberland County and I think there is some confusion over these lists."

Willimina pushed him aside. "That's right. Down in civilized country, we list the places that are off limits, like any sensible person would. What are you trying to pull?"

Now keeping his distance, with his right hand on his pistol, Pinch said, "That's right, in your county we list the waters *closed* to ice fishing. But in Piscataquis County, we list the waters that are *open* to ice fishing. Perch Pond is not on that list. You made a big mistake, Missy Girl Scout Leader, give me your license, lady, so I can write these summonses!" Pinch seemed to be getting his dander up too.

After looking at the horrified scouts and realizing that bad things could happen very quickly, Willimina, still fuming and sputtering, more or less threw her license at Bill who then meekly handed it to Pinch. The warden then commenced to write out two summonses, both in her name. "I'm doing you folks a favor and only writing up you, lady. I could give a summons to each of the adults and most of the kids. But I think you are really the one to blame for this."

"I'll tell you who's to blame!" shouted Willimina. "It's you damned game wardens and your damned biologists and your damned department and your damned legislators! Even a Philadelphia lawyer can't understand all these stupid rules! I sure as hell know Bill here can't and he's as smart as any man I know."

Then she turned to the scouts, the truly shaken Bill and Zapper, and said, "I'll tell you this, if that gd warden doesn't take his hand off that gun of his, there's going to be hell to pay and he'd better know how to shoot it straight because that christly wet behind the ears lad is not going to get a second shot."

She then proceeded to jump up and down as if to break the ice. Pinch looked at Willimina's red flushed face and wild antics and sensed that things might be getting out of control, so he turned to the scouts and told them it was time to pack up their traps and move on back to camp.

Then he handed the summonses to Bill saying, "Give these to the *LADY* when she calms down. I've got more serious matters to attend to." With that he grabbed the container of trout and headed toward his idling snowmobile, being careful to walk directly away from Willimina who was still agitated and stomping up and down to beat the band.

Zappy said he was pretty worried during the whole confrontation. "Not for Willimina, she can take care of herself, that woman for sure. And not for the scouts, they'll see a lot worse later in life. No, Snappy, with or without any witches from Willoby Woods, I was just plumb scared that warden would look in our bait bucket. Who the hell knows if them shiners and mummy chubs I brought up from the coast are legal in this jeesly county. Probably weren't. Besides, I've got a couple of outstanding warrants in this here jurisdiction. Plus I was thinking she might weaken the ice with all that stomping around and put us all in the drink. No, Snap, I don't mind telling you I was some concerned."

After the warden roared off on his snowmobile and with the scouts silent, the adults led them back to the cars and trucks and they all got in. The scouts in particular looked baffled and confused and very worried.

But apparently the life lessons of Willimina Sessions were not about to end just yet. Flaming mad, she was still so agitated that when she got her load of kids and Zapper in the car and started to roar back toward the road with such vehemence her SUV slid off into a snow bank and got stuck. "In fairness to the scouts," Zapper told us, "they were some shook up by all that had happened and one of the kids in the third seat proceeded to freak out." "We're stuck. We're stuck. Oh God, we're stuck," he blurted out. "What if that warden comes back, we'll end up in jail for sure."

Now when Willimina heard that, she ripped around and bellowed, "Shut up, you wimp. What kind of scout are you, son? Haven't your parents ever told you that you are never stuck, never ever stuck, when you have gas in your tank. Now you just sit back and shut up. I got this under control."

"Snappy," Zapper continued, "you had to be there to believe it. For sure. But those kids shut right up and Willa, she proceeded to rock us back and forth, tires spinning and smoking and her holding on to the wheel like there was no tomorrow. But pretty soon we took hold and shot out of that snow drift like we were flying. We got right back on the road and headed back to the camp. Then she turned to the kid in the back and bellowed, 'See? See? What were you worried about? We had a shit load of gas. We are good to go. All your worry and yelling doesn't amount to a piss hole in the snow and I know you know what that is, having seen you make several in the course of this long day on the pond.'"

Zapper said, "Those scouts were silent the entire ride back to camp. When we got there, unloaded and everybody went into the lodge, that's when Bill told Hiram and Peggy. Peggy was real put out for sure. 'We've known Charlie Pinch since he was knee high to a grasshopper and that boy has always been a trial to one and all. This time he went too far, Willimina, I hope you write a few letters. This ain't right. It's really bad for our business. There was no call for that summons. A warning, maybe but the laws should be clearer.'

"'Damn right I will, I'll show that sumbitch he's crossed the wrong scoutmaster this time. I'll eviscerate him,' Willimina said. 'I will destroy that puppy.'"

That night after everybody had dinner and then sat in front of the fire trying to forget what had happened, Willimina went into the kitchen and began to write the first of her series of letters. To the head of the warden service. To the Fish and Game Commissioner. To the Governor. To the *Bangor Daily News*. To the *Bangor Daily News*'s number one outdoor writer, Bud Levitt. She was relentless. We never found out how many letters that woman did finally send off. Apparently they all had a PS which read, "And it's a damn good thing those scouts were around. A man puts his hand on his gun with me around, he'd better be quick and accurate. There was no call for that."

But she did get results. A week later the Commissioner Pemberton Ware himself showed up at Willimina and Gus's house. He brought his reply to her letter. Pemberton acted as if he was the only one she had written to, although he most certainly knew the buckshot blast that she'd sent out hitting him from below and above. He was a fine, old school gentleman that way.

"Ms. Sessions, please let me deliver this letter in person and please accept my apologies. I'm going to rip up these summons and let you keep them as souvenirs. Warden Pinch handled the situation all wrong, that's for certain sure. And he is now reassigned down in Washington County where we have some real malfactors to test his mettle on. Technically, you and the scouts did break the law, but it really was our fault. Why we have different positing rules for one county and another set for others is beyond me. I never realized what a real mess it is. I will make sure we fix it for the next fishing season. That I promise you. I'll make sure we have one list for every single county and I'll tell you, ma'am, I am going to call it 'Willimina's List.' How do you like that?"

Gus told us he'd never seen Willimina so pleased and so tongue tied. She just nodded her thanks, overcome with emotion as she was. "It's a rare time when Willa keeps quiet, for sure. But she was some happy," Gus told us. "She seemed to want to hug Commissioner Pemberton what with the Christmas mistletoe still up over the door and all, but he's pretty light on his feet for an old codger."

Then Gus folded the letter and put it in his pocket as several customers were beginning to gather around. "I got to tell you guys, that wife of mine is a keeper isn't she? I mean she has every right to be proud of herself. I know I am. You know she's not as broad minded as she might be when it comes to trail cams and such, but she really is a pisser when it comes down to that. Some kind of woman. I'm sure a lucky man."

With that he departed and Andre the Giant nodded his approval. "Time to get back to selling," he said, "I don't hear that cash register of mine making no noise. I'll give that Willimina credit though, when she says she's going to kick butt, she sure does kick some serious butt."

And to make sure he kept things moving in the right direction sales-wise, Andre got Gus to give him a copy of the Commissioner's letter. He had that framed and put right over his stock of ice fishing gear adding a big sign which read, "Results? You want results? Get your Cold Boy Tip-ups right here and get results just like Willimina Sessions does."

chapter fourteen

Snow Dance

THERE I WAS, driving south on the Maine Turnpike the Wednesday before Thanksgiving, wondering what the hell I was doing. I love all the holidays, but Thanksgiving is my favorite and I think it is for a lot of hunters. If you've got your deer, it's a great time to wander in the woods, the pressure's off and you feel like quite the superior woodsman.

If you haven't, all those nimrods rushing hither and yon are likely to move more deer around and out of their normal secretive, careful patterns. There are a lot of "lucky" bucks taken over that holiday. Course there's a lot of nimrods blasting away all weekend so it's a tradeoff. I once had two teenagers point their rifles at me as I was still hunting along a gully on Thanksgiving morning. They'd never been hunting before. Not sure they hunted soon after I blistered them unmercifully.

Just being in the woods before the turkey dinner also feels special. You feel a kinship, not to those wretched Pilgrims with their frowning on fun, but with the Indians who got up the idea of a feast for everybody. Not that I ever understood why they treated those interlopers so well. They should have brought poisoned venison and rid the countryside of those dotards. But I suppose even by then it was too late. Still, there was no need to encourage them to stay and prosper.

Anyway, there I was driving south to Hartford, Connecticut, with my family. It is in response to an imperial summons from Sunny's mom, Claire-Marie. She's always been very good about not making many demands on me and very understanding of the needs of guiding, but this was very important to her. Her oldest boy, CJ, was going off to the Marines and she wanted us there for his send-off. We had to come to them so I was doing a good deed and that made me feel better, at least a little better.

Still, I was thinking about Gus and how lucky he was to be heading up to Aroostook County for a big Thanksgiving holiday deer hunt. He knew the county pretty well and often hunted there with Louis Francouer, a legendary Franco American guide who had so many sports signed on, he needed Gus to help him out at the last minute.

How I envied Gus during those long, traffic congested hours as we headed south. I was sure Gus would have a great time and get a deer, if not for himself, at least with one of the sports. Either way he'd end up with a shitload of fine, fresh venison.

The family get-together in Connecticut went reasonably well, but on Sunday as we were driving north, I felt left out and was pretty surly, truth be told, especially when I saw cars and trucks with deer tied to them headed south in the other lanes. The traffic was worse coming back and by the time we got home, it was dark and time for supper. That's when the phone rang. It was Gus. He sounded funny and then he said he wanted to bring over one of my gas cans.

"Don't bother, I'm in a lousy mood," I allowed, but he insisted and soon showed up. The doorbell rang and there he was, all decked out in his black and red wool hunting shirt and in his hand was a big goose. "What the hell?" I exclaimed. He grinned. "You won't believe it. The hunt up in the county blew up so I got home and sat in our blind on the bay, counting my blessings for an hour or so at last light."

"And this goose was your blessing?" I asked incredulously. "Well actually there were two geese. A double. They came into the blind, set their wings, and I got both of them." "No way," I said. "Way," he replied, grinning. "The Goddess of the Hunt rewarded me. Either that or the Goddess of the Golf Course, from which these dumb geese surely came." "For what were you rewarded?" I asked, still incredulous.

"Simply put, Snappy, because the Aroostook hunt was a total fiasco and one or both of those ladies felt some sorry for me. I drove up country for six hours to help Louis Francouer, but it just turned into a hell of a disaster. I stuck it out for four days. Those geese are my reward."

"Well my friend, you bought me a fine goose. Let me get you a glass of something special and you can tell me all about it. I'm feeling better and better. You just got us our Christmas dinner. No pressure on me now."

Gus sat by the fire and I poured him a double measure of his favorite twelve-year-old single malt while he commenced to tell me about his Aroostook hunt.

"Stomper Beaney drove up with me," he began. "It was six hours before we even got into the camp. Louis was in charge of course, and he had four sports for the three of us to take out. Problem was, there was no snow on the ground when we got there. You know the way we always hunt from that camp, each of us takes a sport out the first day. We all set off in different directions and hit the cedar swamps.

"Francouer's whole plan is to have the parties spread out in all directions and find where the deer are coming out of the swamps at last light to feed on the beech mast covering the surrounding areas. Or try to get set up early enough in the morning to ambush them on their way back to the thick cedar. But the trick was always to find which trails they were using during a given period. The deer mixed up their travel plans, just to frustrate us for sure.

"As it happened, we went out early the next morning. It was Sunday so there was no hunting, but we used the time to scout, we thought to good advantage. Louis had divided up the camp chores. Everybody had to pitch in, sports included. By lots, some had to wash the dishes, some had to dig the outside latrine, some had to bring in the wood for the night.

"After our chores were all taken care of, each of us took our sport in a different direction, checking out all the cedar swamps we could. They are usually the key up there. As you know, those deer yards in the winter months where the deer went to avoid the cold winds and to conserve energy in the deep snow. There in the middle of the cedar swamps they get out of the wind, had some crappy food, but at least food in an emergency blizzard. They also conserve energy by walking in each other's trail in the deep snow. So we checked out the runs in and out of the swamps pretty damned closely."

At this point, I'm a little confused as to why Gus is telling a lot of things I already knew but I just nodded like it was all new info and let him run on.

Gus continued, "I had a nice guy from New York for a sport, named Barney, I forget his last name. He was in pretty good shape and he didn't take anything for granted. Barney did what I asked him to do and didn't complain although we walked about ten miles that first day. We found some sign and saw a couple of flags in the distance, but no real patterns, no highways to set up on.

"That afternoon we all got back to the camp and compared strategies and sightings. Among the seven of us, we'd seen maybe four deer. Everybody agreed that without snow, we were going to have a hell of a time locating any real travel patterns. The sports were pretty down. And so were we.

"But Nords Anderson, who was from Mars Hill, and who hunted these parts for a decade or more, swore he could fix things. Of course he'd had a couple of beers and more than a few nips of rum (the drink of choice in Colonial times and the "firewater" of his pretend ancestors), so he might have been seeing things through rose colored glasses, or what they call today beer goggles to be more accurate."

"Now," Gus continued, "you know how most of you guides like to pretend they're like Indians and have real Indian know-how? Well Nords was from the poor part of Mars Hill and his father had been unknown. Somewhere along the line, his grandmother had gone to Canada and had his father up there so there were a lot of questions about his origins. Some said he was part Indian.

"Louis told me that when he grew up, Nords' father was very friendly with the Micmac sachem in the area, so Nords kept thinking he was really at least part Indian. He claimed he was one of the 'People of the Dawn.' Nords tried so hard to be accepted as at least half Indian and claimed that his spirit name was Abenaki for 'Shoots So Straight as to be Unbelievable' or some such. Nords insisted that his wife's Abenaki spirit name was 'She Who Must Be Obeyed,' and that sounded more accurate."

Even today, Nords sure still wanted to be a Micmac and he was always throwing in tribal lingo whenever he could. Maxine, his wife, wasn't much for drinking and kept him on a tight, tight leash most of the year so when he got to hunting camp he let loose in more ways than one.

Gus took another long sip of his drink and continued, "Up in the Aroostook area in those days, there were a couple of tribes, the Micmacs and the Maliseets, both once part of the Abenaki Confederation. The Maliseets had gotten recognized by the Feds as a tribe back in the 1960s and the Micmacs wanted the same.

"They were willing to give anybody claiming to be a Micmac a good look-see as there were only a about a thousand of them at that time and they thought maybe they could use a few more to enlarge the tribe. But Nords was too big a stretch even for them at that time so he never got his personal recognition as an official 'Indian.'

"Anyhow, Nords sure tried hard to 'act Indian' especially when he had a few belts in him. Then Nords would get more and more into his Indian 'past,' and now was no exception. There we were in the middle of the Aroostook wilderness, three guides and four sports and no snow. So Nords decided that his Indian ancestry would be of help so he decided he was going to do his snow dance. Anything to get out of the cabin I said, so we all encouraged him. Even Louis figured it couldn't hurt," Gus said.

Now if you've never spent even one night in a hunting camp, then perhaps you don't know what it can be like but there is something about the body odor, the massive consumption of beans and meat and a bunch of males acting like adolescents all together that creates a real foul and gamey smell. Body odor and foot odor and lots of other odors not for mentioning. It's real gross. Just gross. Then throw in a lot of beer and Jack Daniel's and it's a situation which cries out for cold, fresh air.

Gus shook his head. "I mean now I gotta ask you, Snappy, have you ever seen a jeesly salad in a hunting camp? Never. Bowl of fruit? Same. Fresh vegetables? No way. What you have is a shit load of beans and franks and salt pork and venison if you're lucky or some other kind of meat like baloney or salami or pepperoni. Lots of that. Potatoes, that white bread Sunny hates and a lot of other real junk food? Tons of that. Now you put six or seven guys in a cabin with a stove roaring and you're going to get a lot of overall really foul odor, that's for sure.

"Now Francoer's camp fare is some different when it comes to food. You know that. He does it that good old Franco way. I'm not one for fancy Paris-style cooking but this was real, home style Franco food made for hunters and outdoorsmen, that's for sure. And Louis always laid it on some good.

"Those baked beans smothered in molasses, my lord, even guys who didn't like beans tucked into them some good. We also had a lot of spicy *JoJo* potatoes and *boudin*. Even the cornbread had bacon in it. We had those pork pie things and head cheese, tons of it. I'd have to say that tasted outstanding.

"My favorite was those sweet cakes they call 'Nun Farts,' *Pets de Soeurs*, I think they are called. We ate every last one of those Louis had brought, for sure, and kept asking for more. But all that rich food, well it certainly didn't cut down on the fug, I will have to tell you that as well, Snap." Gus smiled.

"Of course, per usual, one or two of the lads had been saving up farts for the whole year. I mean, they'll tell you their Mrs. at home won't let them cut wind in the house. Why they think we wait all year for them to save up their farts and share them with us, I do not know. Now when Nords wasn't too far in his cups, he'd bring out his lighter and he'd light up some the farts. I mean no TV, so maybe he thought we needed the entertainment. Well that would stop some, but not all, from cutting wind.

"And we all brought sleeping bags which hadn't been cleaned, let alone fumigated, in God knows how long. What a christly smell you can work up in a deer hunting camp in no time flat.

"This friggin' green fog, by the way, is not something you ever see written up in those hunting magazines like *Grey's Sporting Journal*, nor do they feature it on the Outdoor Channel or in that *DownEast* magazine, but you know it's real, Snappy. It's christly real for sure. And it gets realer day by day. Even Francouer came in one day from scouting and said 'Mon Dieu, what an odor.'

"So anyway, Nords took some time putting on his war paint and his Indian costume which really was a buckskin jacket and a few eagle feathers in his hair. He chugged down one more beer and out he went, stopping to put a few pebbles in an old beer can. Then he commenced to doing a chant 'Wa Ka Wa Ka Wee. Wa Ka Wa Ka Wee,' telling the sports was a sacred prayer for snow, good tracking snow, passed down from his dearly departed dad from the inner sanctum of the Micmac sachem's lodge. He said over and over it would always produce the white stuff in abundance. We all took the opportunity to get out of the smelly air of the camp to watch him.

"Well, cold or no cold, didn't he work up a sweat that night, jumping up and down, moving this way and that way, turning and twisting and puffing on a big ceremonial pipe. We all just hoped he wouldn't fall with it in his mouth when he kept stopping from time to time to take yet another libation."

Gus continued, "Now there wasn't much to the chant, 'Wa Ka Wa Ka Wee. Wa Ka Wa Ka Wee,' or its next incarnation, 'Ci Yi Ci Ci Yi,' but he did give it some variations of pitch and emphasis although to me it all came out the same. On and on he went until he finally passed out and fell right into the pucker brush next to the camp. We carried him inside and put him to bed.

"And, don't you know, by the time we all turned in, the moon was gone and the clouds were rolling in. Our hopes were soaring. 'Maybe Nord's snow dance is working,' one of the sports said and part of us wanted to believe it was doing its job. We all went to sleep with hope in our hearts and lots of good old Jack in our bloodstream.

"But when I got up in the middle of the night to take a leak, I found it was already raining some hard. Coming down and drumming on the roof. 'This is not good' I said to myself."

"And it wasn't?" I asked.

"It was still pouring that next day when we woke up.

"We roused Nords and told him what he could do with his christly Snow Dance. 'You dub,' said Louis, 'you total dub. Obviously weren't paying attention when you studied with those Indian ancestors of yours. You learned the Rain Dance, not the Snow Dance.' Nords might have felt bad at being called out like that, but he had such a terrible hangover that all he could do was give Louis a stricken look and put his head back under the pillow and hope to sleep off his splitting headache.

"Louis, with the wisdom of his Acadian ancestors, told one and all the real lesson of all of this over breakfast, 'Don't ever, ever let a Swede do a Snow Dance,' he laughed. 'Unless he's a certified Indian snow dancer and has the papers to prove it. I mean, do not let it happen that rank amateurs get involved in snow making.'

"It continued to rain steadily that night.

"And the next day.

"And the next night.

"What a jeasly turn of events, I tell you," Gus continued, holding up his glass for another refill. "It rained, off and on, but mostly on, for three days. It rained every single day and every single night, washing out any sign any and all deer left.

"Now, Snappy, you know I've only been describing the normal kind of camp fug. The kind you can stand for a day or two, especially if you have a deer or two hanging up. But here you had to add the weather to it. I mean that pouring rain led to misery outside and now inside. With only a few hunters venturing out—and that not for long—and then they come back all wet and smelly and try to dry out their duds. Now you get clouds of vapors from the wool jackets and pants. Vapors upon vapors and more smells than you can shake a stick at."

I smiled as Gus went on. "And the other guys who have been inside all day, well they've been playing cards and drinking beer and Jack Daniel's and eating junk food. I mean, as soon as you come inside, you want to head back out into that christly rain. I did that more than once. Three days and no bathing for the boys. None at all. I did take off with Barney down into a couple of swamps two or three times. But there are only so many hours you can spend in the pouring rain looking for deer who themselves are dead set against moving anywhere at all. The camp air got fouler and fouler.

"That's when the hunt finally blew up, Snappy.

"We guides got together and we all agreed there was no point in all this. The sports themselves looked desperate to go home, looking only for an excuse to end their agony.

Even the fun of lighting farts had lost its luster by then. So finally Louis, seeing all of us about to either lynch Nords or gas him or both said in a loud voice so all the guys with hangovers winced, 'Mes amis, mes amis, Monsieur Stumper has an announcement to make.' With a big shit-eating grin on his face, Stumper surveyed the band of smelly outlaws sitting before him and pronounced, loud and clear, those immortal words you and I first heard from Little Robert those many years ago, but which are now standard lingo for guides of all types and abilities all across our Great State of Maine.

"He stood up and said loudly and firmly, 'Call off the dogs, piss on the fire, this hunt is over.'

"And, Snappy, you know thankfully, it truly was.

"Louis gave us all leave to go if our sports wanted to and to a man-jack they thought some time in a liquor and dance joint would be just the ticket for the rest of their vacation. Forget the deer. Forget the hunt for deer even and switch to an indoor hunt of quiff in a nice warm bar somewhere."

Gus told me one of the sports was from the Bangor area and he said, "I can find you classy tang for every taste and pocketbook, we'll hit the Bounty Tavern and The Showring for grub and then we'll go dancing down in the juke joints by the river. It won't take you ding-dongs three days to score either, I promise you that."

"Sports and guides all thought that was the best idea of the week.

"So we all got the hell out of camp. Pronto.

"Stumper and I beat it back down 95 ahead of just about everybody. I swear it didn't stop raining until we got about to Lincoln and the truck radio said it was clearing up soon, but we were not tempted to go back. I felt like I had been let out of jail. We didn't even dare stop in Bangor in case the sports changed their minds and got an idea to go back. We just headed back to Little Harmony fast as we could go.

"So that's how I came to be sitting in our blind on Thanksgiving when those dumb ass golf course geese came by and committed suicide. When you're sitting down for your Christmas goose dinner, you can thank Nords and his damn Snow Dance. And that is the name of that tune."

And so it was.

Then I didn't feel so bad about missing out on the great Aroostook deer hunt. Spending Thanksgiving with my in-laws actually sounded pretty good in comparison.

Thus ends the first book of tales of Snappy Jack and Big Gus with a repeat of the immortal words of Little Robert:

"Call off the dogs, piss on the fire, this hunt is over."

chapter
fifteen

One Word More

B ut fear not, there will be other hunts and expeditions taking place in the tall pines of Maine, USA, and I hope Big Gus and Snappy Jack will be there to report on them at a later date if there is any interest beyond that of Stevie, Guido, and Dusty. Some additional memory chips already piling up along the blazed trail include

"Flemish Cap Hangover"
"Bob Cat Alibi"
"Tree Killer"
"Cruiser Francouer and the Lynx"
"Poachers I Have Known"
"Snoopy Surfs with the Pollack"
"Pepper Taps True Tang"
"Little Robert Needs Glasses"
"The Ultimate Bear Laxative"
"Little Robert and the Vanishing Hare"

"Bus Stop Buck"

"Hog Tranquilizers for Sale"

"Captain Coombs Irons a Sword"

"Blue Fish Daisy Chain"

"The Happy Tale of the Fisher Cat"

"Shooting Brown Tale Moths for Fun and Profit"

And so on...

Acknowledgments

There are many Maines.

These tales describe but one of them.

THE COLLECTION grew out of some of the stories I was beginning to tell my three grandsons about the hunting and fishing of "yesteryear." Somehow though when my beloved father-in-law, John "Johnnie Q" Quinlan, died, I was moved, even driven, to put those stories down on paper and expand their telling. In the process, characters from the past blended with entirely imaginary characters, central characters faded, and totally new ones would wake me up at 3 a.m., insisting that their story be told. In the process, the work morphed into something else and became more (and less) than simply a set of hunting and fishing tales. It became a paean to the Maine of which I have been fortunate to have been a part for the last forty years. That life in that world has been a true blessing.

Throughout the book I have tried to capture not just hunting and fishing in Maine, but the rural Maine subculture with all its time-honored values and real people, many of whom do not seem to make it into the sporting press. I hope I have stayed true to those men and women who make rural Maine what it truly and authentically is. The portraits and interactions here are meant to be humorous, but they were drawn with love.

I should like to extend my sincere thanks to all those who contributed details, actions, thoughts, names, stories, nuances, experiences, advice, assistance, and additional true tales of their own or who read chapters of various versions: Sumner L. "Sub" Ricker, Anne Springer, James "Jimmy" Shoot, Bill Green, Jason Field, Jennifer Rooks, Sharron Merrill, Bill Utley, John Oliver, David Vail, Juliana L'Heureux, Heather Davis, Alan "Sven" Blum, Rachel Hudson, John Baldacci, Greg Faucher, Carolyn Palombo Clement, "Link" Linkovitch, June Vail, Dan Sullivan, Jewel Bernie LeClaire, Bruce Davis, Robert Boyce, John and Jennifer VerPlanck, Erik Potholm, Sandy Potholm, Dave Emery, Brian Clement, Georgette Miller, Carol Emery, Marty Moore, Fred Hill, Gemma Gatti, Chris Duval, Mark Wethli, Peter Burr, and Samantha Broccoli.

I am also very grateful to those who read the entire manuscript and contributed greatly to its progress and improvement, especially David "Broo" Parmelee, Amy Haible, Keith Brown, and Dick "Cap" Morgan. In addition, Mike Gawtry of L.L.Bean was a tremendous help with his careful reading of each and every dimension of the book and all its various tales. And a huge debt of gratitude also goes to John Christie, "The Marvelous One," for his validation of these stories as reflecting the Maine he has known and loved all of his life.

I really also want to include a heartfelt shout-out to George Smith whose considerable thematic and background input as well as a very generous introduction are greatly appreciated. I welcome his attention to the detail and themes of the collection as much as I have enjoyed hunting and fishing with him since the 1970s. In his many incarnations, George continues to stride across the Great North Woods, indeed across the entire state, as a true son and titan of Maine.

Thanks too need to go to that editor of note at Down East Books, Mike Steere, who offered encouragement, motivation, assistance, and guidance through the publication process and who let the authentic voices of one of the real Maines be heard and his outstanding publisher, Jed Lyons. Jed continues to be an author's best friend to a wider and wider audience with each passing year. They both do an exceptional job. So, too, do their editorial crew led by Karen Ackermann. My thanks to one and all.

Chris Potholm
Harpswell, Maine
2015

Chris Potholm in 1980 during the first Moose Hunt in Maine since 1935